WORM SONGS

When Frankie gatecrashes the local photography club meeting she brings trouble with her. David, Alice and Michael are dragged off to the ruined castle for a night shoot. Tensions mount; but when Alice faints and strange images appear in the photographs, all animosity is forgotten. The investigation into the legendary Borderlands worm has begun...

WORM SONGS

Ann Coburn

CHIVERS PRESS
BATH

First published 1996
by
The Bodley Head Children's Books
This Large Print edition published by
Chivers Press
by arrangement with
The Bodley Head Children's Books
part of Random House UK.
1998

ISBN 0 7540 6018 7

British Library Cataloguing in Publication Data

Coburn, Ann
    Worm songs. – Large print ed. – (The Borderlands
    sequence; 1)
    1. Northumberland (England) – History – Juvenile fiction
    2. Children's stories   3. Large type books
    I. Title
    823.9′14[J]
    ISBN 0 7540 6018 7

For my daughter, Helen,
with all my love

AUTHOR'S NOTE

The Borderlands Sequence is set on the Eastern Border between England and Scotland. I have taken a few historical and geographical liberties with the beautiful town of Berwick upon Tweed, for which I hope my neighbours will forgive me.

The author gratefully acknowledges the financial assistance of *The Society of Authors*.

'History is a pattern of timeless moments.'

T.S. Eliot

CHAPTER ONE

They came for her in the brightest part of the day when the sun had cleared the dark bulk of Worm Hill and was warming the walls of the village houses below. Martha sat in her open doorway, dressed in her best skirt and petticoats, wrapped in her warmest plaid. She was waiting for them. She had been waiting for days.

Still, Martha thought of running. She listened to the jingling harnesses and the soft clump of hooves on the dirt road and her mouth turned as dry as chalk. She looked towards the welcoming shadows of the forest at the base of Worm Hill. She could be amongst the trees before they rounded the bend...

Then, little Jennet coughed. Martha frowned as she heard the wet rattle sounding above the barefoot scuffling of the villagers. Every year, Jennet's cough returned with the damp autumn evenings, but this year it was early. Out of habit, Martha looked into her cottage, searching for the leather pouch of coltsfoot leaves.

1

But there were no pouches hanging from her rafters now. All that remained were the darker streaks where oils and sap from drying plants had stained the wood.

Martha drew a deep breath, taking in the fading scents of peppermint and cloves. Jennet would go without her coltsfoot syrup this winter, which meant that she might not see the spring. The thought made Martha angry. She turned her back on the forest and stood her ground.

There were six men on horseback. The last rider was leading another horse. This horse had no saddle, only a thick coil of rope looped around its neck. Martha saw how they meant to take her, and her anger grew.

The captain slid from his horse and pushed past her into the cottage. It was a small cottage, sparsely furnished. It did not take long to search.

'Where is the child?' he asked, stooping as he came back out of the low doorway.

'My daughter? Gone,' said Martha, pleased to hear how calm and clear her voice sounded.

The captain grunted. He had expected

2

no other answer.

'And your poisons, your books of spells?'

Martha looked bewildered. 'Sir?' she said.

The captain turned away and growled a word of command. One of the men came towards her with the rope. He kept his eyes down. Martha waited until he was reaching for her before she spoke.

'Joseph,' she said. 'You are not limping, I see. I told you my salve was good.'

Joseph choked off a reply and reached for her again.

'And your mother?' she asked.

Joseph threw a desperate look at his captain.

'No more fevers?'

Joseph groaned, dropped the rope at her feet and turned away. With a curse, the captain picked up the rope.

'Wait! On whose orders do you take me?'

The captain sighed. 'The orders of Sir Robert, Lord of the East March,' he recited. 'He has the papers, from the Privy Council.'

'And the charge?'

3

'You know the charges, witch.'
'Tell me.'
'That you did use foul potions and charms to bewitch his son, James. And...'
'Yes,' prompted Martha.
'That you did use evil spells and songs to awaken the worm,' muttered the captain, unable to resist one wary glance at Worm Hill.

A frightened whisper shivered through the villagers like a cold breeze. Martha nodded, satisfied.

'There is no need to truss me like a beast to market' she said, swinging herself up onto the horse. 'I shall ride to—to...'

'To the castle dungeons,' snarled the captain, trying to salvage some control. Martha turned pale with fear but she made herself hold his gaze.

'I will ride with you to the castle. You have my word.'

'Aye, let her ride!' shouted Jennet's mother and the crowd murmured agreement.

The captain hesitated. He knew how a crowd could turn.

'You have my word,' said Martha.

The captain shrugged, climbed back on

4

to his horse and gave the lead reins a vicious tug. Even this small victory was used against her, later.

CHAPTER TWO

At first, Alice barely noticed the long, dark shadow spreading across the grass from the castle ruins. She had stopped on the road into town and was leaning over the wall which hemmed the valley top, deep in thought. On the far side of the wall the land sloped steeply, falling away to the valley floor. A path zig-zagged through the grass all the way down to the river, passing the dark lump of the ruins on the way. Alice gazed down into the valley without looking directly at the crumbling stonework of the ruins. She was afraid of high, dangerous places.

The ruins were all that was left of a grand Borders castle. The Victorians had driven the East Coast main line right through it and poached most of the stone to build a station. Only one tower was left standing, and one great wall clinging to the valley side. A steep flight of stone steps, known as break-neck stairs, edged up the face of the wall, stopping short of the tower. The top step hung over a sheer drop to the rocks and nettles below.

The shadow from the ruins was growing all the time, edging up the slope towards her, but still Alice would not look. She switched her gaze over to the left, where the railway station stood. The Edinburgh train was pulling in. Alice watched as the commuters piled out onto the platform, lifting their faces to the early evening sun and shaking the day from their shoulders before heading home. Home! Alice groaned. Home was the last place she wanted to be.

Below her, the shadow cast by the ruins had ballooned to an impossible size. The shape was changing and the darkness was thickening to a deep black. Alice was busy frowning down at her long, skinny arms as they rested on the warm sandstone wall. Her elbows stuck out on either side as sharp as javelins. Her long, black hair poured forward over her shoulders and collected in a dark pool on the top of the wall. Alice scowled. She did not want to be tall and skinny with dark, straight hair. She wanted to be small, with fair, curly hair, like the rest of her family.

With a sigh, she reached into her pocket and pulled out the photograph, the one that had been taken on her last birthday. There she was, sitting in the big, squashy armchair. Her mum and step-dad were stooped behind the chair, with their heads resting on the back like two coconuts on a shy. The twins, Gary and Kevin, knelt on the floor in front of her, leaning together and smiling their identical smiles. She looked like a great, dark cuckoo stuck in a nest of fluffy little sparrows.

The train left the station and soared out over the river on the high back of the Royal Border Bridge. For a second, Alice wished she was on it, but then she shook her head. Running away was for cowards like her real dad, who had disappeared before she was even born.

Just then, the darkness from the castle ruins finally reached the top of the wall where she stood and slid across her arm like a cold hand. Alice jumped and lifted her head. Her mouth dropped open as she stared at the slope below. Her brain refused to accept what her eyes were seeing. A huge, square, turreted shadow lay across the whole of the valley side.

Alice froze. She dared not turn her head to look at the ruins. She did not want to see a towering castle instead of one crumbling wall. As long as she did not look, she could pretend that the shadow was a cloud over the sun, so she stood like a statue and waited for the shadow to disappear.

The shadow stayed. Its edges became clearer with every passing second. Then the roar of cars on the road behind her began to grow faint. For a minute everything was quiet. Alice held her breath, waiting for the next car. Instead she heard the muffled clump of approaching hooves. A horse snorted. A woman cried softly.

Alice began to shake. The horses were directly behind her now. The woman was close enough for Alice to hear her take a shaky breath. Then the woman spoke.

'Help me, child,' she said.

Alice blocked her ears against the

voice. A hand gripped her arm and she screamed.

'Hey! What's wrong?'

It was David. Frantically, Alice twisted to face him. As she turned, the air filled with the drone of cars once more and the shadow retreated from the valley side.

'Oh, David! David, the castle!'

David squinted down into the valley. 'What? The ruins? What about them?'

'Don't they look sort of—bigger?'

David glanced down the hill again. 'No.'

Alice took courage from his answer and risked one quick look. There were the ruins, one tower, one wall, the same as always. All the air rushed out of her in a gasp of relief.

She turned back to David, already feeling slightly foolish. 'Um, they—grew,' she muttered.

David raised his eyebrows. 'Into what?'

'Into a castle.'

David's eyebrows shot up even higher. He folded his arms and stared at Alice. It was a two-mile bike ride from his farm to the edge of town, but his thick, fair hair looked as though it had just been combed. His bike gleamed in the evening sunshine, as clean and shiny as on the day it had left the shop. His camera bag was strapped neatly into place behind the saddle. He looked so solid and ordinary that suddenly Alice wanted to laugh. Fiercely, she swallowed down a giggle.

'Are you telling me you just saw the ruins grow into a castle?'

'Not exactly. I didn't dare to look at the ruins. But the shadow—it was huge...'

'Oh, well,' said David. 'That's easily explained. It's because the sun is so low. Everything's throwing long shadows, see?'

'Yes, but ...' Alice pointed at the steady stream of cars on the road beside them. 'All the traffic stopped. Just for a minute.'

'That would be the traffic lights,' said David, patiently.

'But—I heard horses behind me instead of cars. And there was ...' Alice saw the look of astonishment on David's

10

face and trailed to a feeble stop without mentioning the woman's voice. 'It ... it was as if I'd—gone back in time. Well, that's what it felt like.'

David chose his words carefully. 'Alice, are you sure you're up to going to the photography club meeting tonight? Perhaps, if you're not feeling well ...?'

At last, the tension of trying to explain something she did not understand became too much. The giggles came bubbling out.

'Don't look so worried, David,' she spluttered. 'I'm having another cuckoo day. That's probably all it is.'

David gave her a relieved smile. Cuckoo days he could understand. Alice had told him all her worries about her different looks.

'Oh, that again,' he said, grabbing his bike by the handlebars and setting off down Border Road into town.

'Yes, that's all it was,' said Alice, following.

*   *   *

At the bottom of the hill the evening sun

11

brought a glow to the red rooftops of the old, walled part of town where the buildings crowded together on their little square of land, bounded on three sides by the river, the harbour and the sea. Border Road was even older than the town walls. It ran from the main wall gate straight up the valley side, and the newer part of town had grown up along the length of it. First, there were the solid, Victorian houses with their ranks of chimney stacks, then, further out, the orderly grids of housing estates and small factory units.

'Old and New,' said David, nodding down the hill at the town. 'That could be the title for our next exhibition project. Plenty of locations down there, look. What do you think?'

'Great,' said Alice, watching the rolling sea and smelling the salt air. It was good to be out. Suddenly, it was so good to be out, Alice had to run. She pelted down the street as far as Michael's house then grabbed a lamp post to stop herself. She swung round the base so fast her feet left the ground.

David caught up with her, trundling

his bike. 'Are you on for a shared project again, then?' he said, as though nothing had happened.

'Great,' panted Alice.

'OK, I'll check it out with Michael.'

'You know he'll say yes,' said Alice. 'He always agrees with everything we say.'

'Still, it's only right to ask,' said David, who liked to do things properly.

'Go on, then,' said Alice, nodding up at the old, stone-built house where Michael lived. 'You can ask him when you call for him.'

David propped up his bike, folded his arms and raised his eyebrows. 'You know it's your turn, Alice. I did it last time.'

'Oh, go on, David. Please?'

David shook his head. 'It's your turn.'

'But you're so much better with you-know-who than I am.'

'It's your turn, Alice.'

Alice sighed and frowned at the bay window of the main room of Michael's flat. All the blinds were down, as usual. Mr Adams liked his privacy. Alice shivered as she climbed the steps to the

13

front door and pressed the buzzer.

'Yes?' crackled the voice of Michael's father from the intercom. 'Who is it?'

Alice rolled her eyes. Mr Adams knew very well who was at the door. They called for Michael to go to photography club at the same time every week, and every week Mr Adams asked who it was at the door.

'Why can't he wait for us on the doorstep?' she grumbled, even though she already knew the answer. Michael's father thought that waiting on doorsteps was common. Michael's father expected Michael's friends to call for him properly. Alice could not understand why Mr Adams insisted on this, since he never seemed to enjoy having visitors.

Alice sighed again, then pressed the intercom button and leaned forward. 'It's me, Alice. Alice Mitchell.' She kept her voice polite, for Michael's sake.

The front door lock was released. Alice walked through into the hallway, took a deep breath and pushed open the door of Michael's flat.

'Good evening, Alice,' said Mr Adams from the sofa. 'How are you?'

'Fine,' she said. 'Thank you.' She hovered by the door, hoping that he would not ask her to sit down. There was only the sofa, which was white and very clean, like everything else in the room.

'Come in, Alice. Come in.'

Alice took a few more steps into the room, treading carefully so that her trainers would not scuff the polished wooden floor. She came to a stop well away from the white wool rug and glanced along the passageway towards Michael's room, willing him to hurry up.

'Michael will be out shortly,' said Mr Adams.

Alice nodded. 'Thank you,' she said, again.

The silence grew.

'Are you doing anything ... interesting ... at your photography club?'

'Old and New,' blurted Alice. 'That's our next exhibition project. We're going to take photographs of places around town where old and new things stand together.'

'Really?' Mr Adams turned his gaze on Michael, who had slipped quietly into

15

the room while Alice was talking. 'Michael? Why didn't you tell me about your new project?'

'Oh, Michael doesn't know about it yet, Mr Adams.'

'Aha.' Mr Adams was still looking at Michael, who was looking at his feet. 'Do your . . . friends . . . decide everything for you, Michael?' His tone was pleasant but his eyes were hard.

Alice glanced at Michael and saw that the corner of his mouth was beginning to twitch. 'Well, Mr Adams, when I say next project, I mean if Michael wants to do it. We haven't talked to him about it yet.'

'Aha. Michael? What do you think?'

'Yes,' whispered Michael.

'Would you like to expand on that, Michael?'

The deepening silence was broken by the buzzing of a fly. Trapped between the blind and the window, it was frantically beating against the pane. Alice knew how the fly felt. After a few minutes in that still, white room, she, too, wanted to run to the window and smash her way through to the sunshine outside. Mr

Adams swivelled his head, searching out the fly, and Michael, released from his father's stare, made a break for the front door.

'Well, Mr Adams,' said Alice, in a bright, loud voice, 'We'd better go now, or we'll be late.' She hurried after Michael.

'You can tell me all about it when you get back, Michael,' called Mr Adams, as Alice stepped into the hallway, rubbing at her goose-pimply arms. She always felt cold in Michael's flat. It reminded her of a huge, white fridge. She pulled the door shut and imagined all the lights clicking off in the room behind her, leaving Mr Adams sitting, preserved, on the white sofa, in the humming darkness, until Michael opened the door again.

Alice shuddered and ran out into the street. Poor Michael. She came up beside him and tried to link her arm through his, but Michael flinched away with a stiff little smile. Idiot! she thought, moving past Michael to walk beside David. Now he'll have to start again.

She meant the ritual. Every time Michael left the flat, he went through the same, strict sequence of actions. First, he took the key ring from his pocket and then he counted the keys on it, twice, to make sure they were all there. If the keys did not slide smoothly through his fingers for the counting, then he would have to start again. It was vital that the keys were back in his pocket before he reached the church, for then his hand had to be free to tap every one of the railings as he passed. If he missed a railing, he had to start again.

Alice understood that this ritual was something Michael needed to go through. It was his way of leaving his father behind. Once past the church, when the flat was out of sight, Michael would relax and catch up with them. Until then, Alice and David always walked slightly ahead and left him to it. Whatever Michael had to do to get by was fine with them.

But sometimes Alice felt like murdering Mr Adams.

CHAPTER THREE

The photography club meeting was nearly over when the door of the wooden hut flew open. Everybody jumped. Mrs Gordon had been droning through her closing remarks like a bumblebee and the room was warm, so even the most determined listeners were more than half asleep when the door handle hit the wall with a splintering crash. Alice turned to look and blinked at what she saw.

A tiny girl stood in the doorway. Her skin was black, her hair was full of stars and her clothes would not have been out of place in a circus. She would have caused a stir anywhere. In a hut in the car park of the local community centre, she was an astonishment. Everybody gaped as though a unicorn had just walked in.

The girl grinned and made a neat turn. The stars in her hair and the buckles of her roller boots glittered under the fluorescent lights.

'Can I help you, dear?' droned Mrs Gordon, after a short silence.

The girl glided into the room. Alice listened to the roller blades trundling across the wooden floor, entranced.

'Is this it? Is this the film club?' asked the girl, in a high, clear voice. She had an unmistakable American accent. Alice hugged herself. An American accent! This was getting better and better.

'We are the Borders photography club, dear.'

'That too,' said the girl, sliding into one of the empty chairs in the front row.

'You—want to join us?'

'Sure do.'

'Well, dear, that is wonderful. I'm always pleased to see young people finding hobbies to keep them off the stree—'

'Hobby?' interrupted the girl. 'Hobby? I'm going to be the greatest film director ever. I'm not into hobbies.'

Mrs Gordon's eyes bulged.

'Perhaps you'd like to stand up and introduce yourself to the group.'

'Love to. Um, OK. You already know about the greatest film director thing. I'm from California. We got here yesterday and we're staying for a year.

20

My dad's a geophysicist. He's really into researching earthquakes, but there's not much money in that, so he'll be working for Triton Fuels off the coast here, looking for oil. Any questions?'

'Thank you, dear,' Mrs Gordon shouted over the laughter. 'Why don't you join the other children? I'm sure they'd let you be part of their project. "Old and New", isn't it ...?'

The girl followed Mrs Gordon's pointing finger to the back of the room, where Alice, David and Michael sat. Gracefully, she cruised towards them. David folded his arms and scowled. Michael's fingers began a nervous dance up and down the buttons of his jacket. Alice's grin grew even broader as she watched this wonderful girl skate towards her. The girl met her eyes and grinned back.

'Hi,' she said. 'I'm Frankie. Come with me.'

*   *   *

'There.' Frankie stood back with a proud smile.

21

Alice felt her heart sink. Frankie had led them up Border Road to the exact spot where she had stood earlier in the evening. She thought of the woman's voice and shivered.

'OK. So, what you need to do now is look where I'm pointing,' said Frankie, sarcastically.

Reluctantly, Alice moved to the wall and looked down at the river.

'No! Not there! There! See?' Frankie stabbed her finger over to the left, halfway down the slope, where the castle ruins stood dark against the pale evening sky.

'The ruins,' said Alice, without looking.

Frankie turned impatiently, making her blades scrape and spark against the wall. 'Naw. The whole thing!'

Alice glanced at Michael for help, but he was busy twisting his buttons and watching David push his bike up the road.

The whole thing? Alice made herself look, scanning the dark lump of the ruins, the bright station platform and the silver rail tracks running between them.

'It's perfect,' crowed Frankie.

David caught up with them. His face was red. His mouth was set in a tight line. 'Right,' he grated, 'What couldn't wait?'

'Hen's teeth! Can't you see it? The castle ruins? The station cosying up alongside? The river running below?'

'So?'

'Gimme a break. You can't be that stupid.'

David grabbed his bike and started to walk away.

'Old and new!' called Frankie. 'For the project. See, you've got three different times all in one place! There's the river, right? That's ancient. And those ruins look pretty old to me. Then you've got a bang up-to-date main line railway—'

David stopped, turned. 'You think you can come into our town, where we've lived all our lives—'

'So far,' interrupted Frankie with a grin.

'—and show us something we don't already know?'

'Well, I hadn't thought of it,' said Alice and wilted under David's glare.

23

'I had,' said David. 'But I was waiting for our meeting. That's how we always do it. We have our meeting and we decide where to shoot. That's how we always do it.'

Michael nodded.

'But look at that skyline! Why not shoot some film now?'

'You do what you want.'

'Aw, come on! I told you, we only moved in yesterday. My camera's still packed away with the rest of my stuff. Hey, loan me yours, Davey. I'll be careful.'

'Don't call me Davey,' hissed David, moving off.

'All right. All right, then,' said Frankie, skating up behind him. Deftly, she unhooked the elastic luggage strap at the back of his bike and snatched the camera case. Then she raced off down the zig-zag path towards the ruins.

They stood, stunned, listening to her wheels rumbling on the tarmac. David winced at the edgy, higher note as the blades took the first turn in the path.

'She's got my camera,' he whispered. 'She's got my camera!'

David seemed unable to move. He gripped the handlebars of his bike as though someone might try to snatch that away too.

'I'll go,' said Alice.

She ignored the path, instead plunging straight down the slope. It was the only way to catch up before Frankie took the last bend in the path and shot down the final stretch into the river. Already, Frankie was going too fast to be in control but she seemed to have no fear. She was leaning into the wind for even more speed and whooping with excitement.

Alice stretched her long legs and went faster, grateful for the way her new trainers gripped the slippery grass. She was scared and angry but, even as she careered towards the bench at the final turn, she found herself grinning wildly.

As the bench loomed up, Alice leaned back, digging her heels into the hillside and shortening her steps. She cannoned into the bench with seconds to spare. Frantically, she turned her back on Frankie, hooked her right arm and leg around the bench-end and stuck her left

25

arm out into the path.

'Yaaaaay!' yelled Frankie as she grabbed at Alice. Her nails dug in and Alice was yanked off her feet. They swung in a dizzy arc and slammed into the bench together before falling on to the grass with all the breath knocked out of them.

'If you've broken my camera …' yelled David from above them. Alice and Frankie looked up to see him trundling his bike down the twisting path as fast as he could. Michael scurried beside him.

'The camera …' Alice sat up and gazed around her, relaxing when she saw the case resting in the grass a few feet away.

'The cycle comes too?' giggled Frankie.

'Look, his bike means a lot to him. And that camera—'

'Sad,' grinned Frankie, unclipping her roller boots. 'Come on.' She ran through the grass in her socks, scooped up the camera and headed for the ruins.

'Hey!' yelled Alice, jumping to her feet. 'You know you'd be in the river now, if I hadn't stopped you …?'

26

'But you did stop me,' sang Frankie, without looking round. Alice shook her head and followed, wincing as a bolt of pain shot through her right shoulder.

The castle ruins loomed over them as they stood at the bottom of break-neck stairs. Alice tried very hard to keep her head down, but the stairs tugged her gaze upwards, step by step, until she was peering at the very top slab which jutted out into space high above her. As she stood with her head tilted back, the ground gave a sudden lurch and the slab rocked against the sky. Alice gasped, dropped her gaze and turned away as a familiar sick dizziness swept over her, but still she staggered and would have fallen but for the wall at her back.

Alice closed her eyes and waited for her head to clear. It was an old problem, this fear of heights, and she knew how to deal with it. She slowed her breathing and thought about flat beaches and smooth bowling greens until the ground felt solid once more.

When she opened her eyes again, the gloom had deepened in the shadow of the wall. The sun was setting on the other side of the ruins and the tower blocked out any light from the station. The damp, musty smell of old stone was everywhere. Alice jumped when the tannoy system at the station blared briefly.

'Spooky,' she muttered, moving well away from break-neck stairs. Frankie ignored her, intent on taking photographs.

'I said, it's spooky here.'

'Uh-huh,' said Frankie, jamming David's camera against the wall with the lens pointing skyward.

'Careful with that!'

'Uh-huh,' said Frankie again, shooting film as fast as the shutter speed would allow. There was a September chill in the air and the evening dew was soaking into her socks, but Frankie paid no attention to the cold or her wet feet.

'Uh-huh, uh-huh. You sound just like my mum when she's really into a book.'

Frankie rushed past Alice and began moving crab-wise around the base of tower, shooting all the while.

'Come on, Frankie. He'll be here any minute...'

'Uh-huh...'

Alice gave up and turned her back to watch for David. He had stopped to chain his bike to the bench. Alice winced, seeing how boring he must look to Frankie. She glanced back at the ruins expecting a mocking hoot, but Frankie was still busy with the camera.

'Look, she hasn't harmed it—' Alice began, as David ran up, but David pushed straight past her, his eyes fixed on Frankie. Alice had never seen him so angry.

'She shouldn't've done that,' said Michael, coming up behind her.

'It's OK. It's not broken or anything,' said Alice, giving him a reassuring smile, but Michael looked at her with eyes as round and blank as the eyes of a frightened bird.

'She shouldn't have,' he repeated, his voice quivering.

Alice sighed and followed David. He had rescued his camera case from the grass and was making a great show of wiping it dry, but the performance was lost on Frankie.

'Great camera, Davey,' she called.

29

'Give it back,' said David, holding out his hand.

'In a mo'.'

'Now,' said David.

Frankie hopped onto break-neck stairs and skipped up the first few steps, leaving wet, black footprints in the dust. Alice stared at the footprints and frowned as a chill ran through her.

'Nearly done,' sang Frankie, still snapping.

'Now!' roared David, lunging at the steps and grabbing for Frankie. He caught her around the ankle and pulled. Frankie staggered back to the edge of the stairs. She flung out her arms, windmilling for balance, and the camera flew from her hand.

Alice started running as soon as she saw the camera arc over David's head. She had a natural catcher's eye, which, combined with her height, had won her a place on the netball first team at school. Even as she sprang forward, Alice was automatically calculating angles and distances. She stretched out her hand and the camera dropped into her palm with a satisfying slap.

Triumphantly, she turned to David, holding the camera high, and a door clicked open behind her. Alice stopped. She knew there were no real doors in the dank gloom beneath the wall, but there was no other way to describe what was happening. Some sort of doorway was opening behind her, she could feel it.

Alice had come across some bad doors in her time, and each one had a colour. There was the door her real father had walked out of before she was born. Grey was how she pictured that one. Grey and sealed, with no handle. Then there was the glitter of frosted glass at the dentist's surgery, dark wood panels for the head teacher's study and a bright yellow door to the back room where the vet had silenced her cat, Chance, after the accident. But this door ... A warning shiver hummed along her spine. This door had all those colours and more.

The opening widened and suddenly the air was thick with hate. Something was looking to do harm. Alice wanted to run but was almost too frightened to move. With a great effort, she turned her head to look at Michael. At first he met

31

her gaze with a puzzled smile, then it seemed to reach him, too. His smile faded, his head went up and his eyes grew wide.

'... Dad ...?' he said.

Alice gasped and clenched at the camera which began to whir, breaking up the darkness with spasms of white light. In fits and starts she saw Frankie, still teetering, her arms flailing, she saw David's shocked white face and she saw the wet, black footprints on the steps. The footprints! Alice nearly screamed. She closed her eyes and made her hand unclench. The flashing light stopped and she held her breath in the sudden darkness, hoping to be overlooked.

'Help me, child.'

Alice gasped and opened her eyes. Two blood-smeared hands were reaching out of the darkness. Alice tried to step back but found she could not move. Horrified, she waited for the hands to grab her. But they came to a sudden halt, held back by stout, iron bars. A white face thrust itself up against the bars. Two huge, dark eyes stared out at her.

'Help me,' pleaded the woman.

'She's trapped!' shrieked Alice.

Michael thought Alice must mean Frankie. He squinted through the gloom and saw Frankie feeling her way down the steps.

'Frankie's safe, Alice,' he called.

'She's trapped! She can't get out!'

Michael turned and saw that Alice was not looking at Frankie. Alice was staring into the darkness at something only she could see. He felt the skin on the back of his neck pull tight. 'Alice ... ?' he breathed.

Alice opened her mouth, but no sound came out. Then her eyes rolled up in her head until only the whites were showing and she fell onto the wet grass at his feet.

CHAPTER FOUR

'Come on, tell me.'

Alice groaned and pedalled harder, trying to leave Frankie behind, but Frankie had the better bike. She simply changed gear and stayed alongside.

'Alice. Tell me. Why did you pass out?'

'I've told you a billion times! I'm scared of heights. I looked up at break-neck stairs and I went dizzy.'

'No. I don't buy it. You were more than dizzy. I saw you, Alice. You were scared out of your wits! Something happened, right?'

Alice scowled. It was Saturday, four days since the night at the castle, and still she was no nearer to understanding what had happened.

'And Michael was real edgy,' continued Frankie. 'He wasn't nearly as scared as you were, but—'

'Michael doesn't like fights, that's all. He gets—upset. You shouldn't have taken David's camera.'

'Yeah, but—'

'Look, just shut up about it, all right?' Grimly, Alice cycled on. She knew Frankie was right about Michael. He had sensed something, but apparently he wanted to keep it to himself. Alice had caught one glimpse of him at school, as he detoured into the boys' toilets to avoid meeting her in the corridor.

For David, the explanation was simple. It was all Frankie's fault. She had caused the fight which upset Michael. She had taken Alice to break-neck stairs and made her faint. David said Frankie was a troublemaker and Alice had not argued. She knew David would only raise his eyebrows if she told him about the evil which had invaded the darkness below the wall. She knew he would simply fold his arms and give her his patient, superior look if she added that every night since then she had dreamed. In the dream she was standing, frozen, at the top of break-neck stairs, watching the wet, black footprints glisten on the steps below.

Each night, the footprints were one step nearer.

Alice shuddered, remembering. No, only Michael would understand. He had felt the wrongness, too. She would talk to him today, after the meeting. Until then, Frankie would get nothing out of her.

'Alice, are you reading me? Come in please...'

'Look Frankie, David doesn't want

35

you around after what you did on Tuesday night. You're only coming to this meeting because I stuck up for you and I'm beginning to wish I hadn't bothered. Shut up about the castle and get behind me. We've got to turn right here.'

They veered off the road into a narrow lane. Alice pulled over and straddled her bike.

'That's where we're going,' she said, as Frankie pulled up beside her.

Ahead of them, the lane sloped gently, running down through a mile of farmland to the river. On either side of the lane fields spread out, freshly ploughed after the harvest and already covered with a green mist of new growth.

'David's farm,' said Alice, sweeping her arm over the fields. 'And there's the house.' She pointed down to the end of the lane where a solidly-built farmhouse overlooked the river. Behind the house a fat grain silo towered over the clustered barns like a giant oxygen cylinder. Sunlight bounced off the shiny sides of the silo and made the sandstone walls of the house glow a soft pink.

Frankie whistled. 'Pretty.'

'Isn't it?' said Alice, smiling proudly. She loved David's farm almost as much as he did.

'So, what happened at the castle?' said Frankie.

Alice stopped smiling. 'Look, for the ten billionth time—'

'She's trapped! That's what you said. She's trapped! Michael felt something. You saw someth—'

'—nothing. I saw nothing.' Alice pushed off without looking at Frankie. 'Let's go.'

Alice cycled off down the lane, her long black hair flying out behind her. Frankie sat back in her saddle, narrowing her eyes to watch Alice go.

'Uh-huh,' she said.

*   *   *

Michael was already there. Alice gave him a smile as she climbed up into the loft, but he missed it. After one quick glance in her direction, he had gone back to pouring fixative solution into a tray.

'Hi, guys,' called Frankie from below.

37

Michael jumped and the liquid overshot the tray, sloshing onto the bench.

David grabbed a fistful of tissues from a nearby box and mopped up the mess. 'Did you have to bring her?' he hissed.

'Don't start that again,' whispered Alice.

'You just want another girl around.'

That hurt. Alice opened her mouth to retort, but shut it again as Frankie's head popped up through the hatch. David blinked as the rest of Frankie emerged into the loft. She was wearing a silver top and leggings, a gold sequined waistcoat and Doc Marten boots sprayed with metallic paint. She had clipped a scattering of silver lightning bolts into her hair.

'Anyone got any sunglasses?' muttered David.

Frankie grinned at him. 'Am I too bright for you, Davey?' She turned, inspecting the loft. 'Hey! Neat darkroom!'

'Don't touch anything,' warned David, as Frankie headed for the benches.

'I'll be careful.'

'That's what you said about my camera and look at this!' David held out his camera, pointing out the dull scrapes marking the glossy black surface.

'Yeah but the camera's OK. That's just the outside.'

'It's scratched.'

'You think that's scratched? Look at mine.' Frankie delved into her bag and pulled out the most battered camera David had ever seen. 'See? Still works.'

'You scratched my camera,' said David. 'You should say sorry.'

Frankie gave him a big smile. 'Yeah, sure, if that's what you want. I'm real sorry, Davey.' Without waiting for a reply, she walked over to see what Michael was doing at the bench.

David clenched his fists. The camera was spoiled for him. Every time he picked it up, the rough edges of those scratches caught at his fingers. It hurt him even to look at his camera now, but Frankie could not see the harm she had done. She was making his complaints look silly. Well, he was going to make her look silly soon enough!

David yanked the ladder up into the

loft, closed the hatch, flicked off the main light and left them all standing in the dark. He waited for a few seconds, hoping Frankie would call out, but she stayed silent until he switched on the red bulb in the corner of the loft.

'Hey, great! You're developing something?'

'That's right,' said David. He opened the back of his camera, took out the film and held it up for Frankie to see. 'Tuesday night at the castle.'

Frankie's smile disappeared. 'Now wait just one minute,' she said. 'How good are you at this developing game? I don't want my film ruined.'

Slowly, David lowered his hand. His face was a dull crimson in the glow from the bulb. When he spoke his voice came from deep in his throat.

'Your film ...?'

Michael edged into a corner and pressed his back against the wall.

'Tell her, David,' said Alice. 'About the developing...'

'I've been doing my own film for nearly a year now and—'

'—Yeah, but is he any good?'

40

interrupted Frankie, her anxiety over the photographs making her blind to David's growing fury. 'I mean, there's some excellent work on that film—'

'You're serious, aren't you?' David glared at Frankie. 'Five minutes of flinging my camera around in bad light and you think you've got the photograph of the century in here...'

'Possibly.'

'They'll all be rubbish!' roared David.

Frankie blinked, then recovered. 'A few, maybe—'

'All of them!'

Frankie narrowed her eyes and drew herself up as tall as her tiny frame would allow. 'Uh-huh,' she said. 'OK. Go ahead.'

*   *   *

'Not bad,' said Frankie, an hour later, inspecting the line of prints hung up to dry.

'Not bad?' said Alice. 'They're brilliant.'

'Oh, yeah,' said Frankie. 'The prints are good. When I said not bad, I was talking about the developing.'

David turned from the bench. The look on his face made Michael snigger nervously.

'So, Davey. See any rubbish?' asked Frankie, waving her hand at the line of prints.

'I haven't finished the film yet,' growled David. 'Still one to go.'

Alice raised her eyebrows at Michael, who sniggered again. She could see how much the tension was getting to him. His shoulders were hunched and his gaze darted between David and Frankie, but they were too busy fighting to notice. Alice had long since given up trying to referee.

'Yeeesss!' said David, gazing into the developing tray. 'I see rubbish appearing!'

'What?' said Frankie.

'Oh, yes. It's getting clearer. Look at that! Out of focus, finger over the shutter—'

'Aw, come on. That's basic stuff. I'd never—'

'Ru-ub-bish!' crowed David. 'I see rubbish!'

Frankie rushed over and stared down at the developing print.

'That's not mine,' she said, glaring across the tray at David.

'It is,' said David, glaring back.

'Not.'

'Is!'

'Not!'

'Um,' said Alice, peering over Frankie's shoulder. 'I think that was me—'

'—Is! You used the whole film. *My* whole film.'

Alice tried again. 'No, that's my shot. I took it by accident. Remember, when I caught the camera ...?'

'—Still on about your lousy film? You are one mean guy, Davey,' said Frankie, scrabbling in her bag. 'Here,' she thrust two new films at him. 'Have one on me.'

Alice sighed and looked down at the tray. The print was darkening rapidly. 'Oh, it's over-developing. David, the print...'

David pushed Frankie's hand away. 'Don't call me mean, you thief!'

Alice rolled her eyes and grinned across at Michael, but he ignored her

43

too. He was standing absolutely still, staring into the developing tray. Even in the dull red glow of the darkroom, she could see that his face was as white as his father's wool rug.

'Look,' he said, and his voice was strangely distant.

They all peered down into the tray. The print was completely black now, apart from a lighter square at the centre. Alice watched, expecting the square to blacken and fade. Instead it grew brighter. She stepped back, feeling her skin turn cold.

'What is that?' asked Frankie. 'Do you see that?'

'Some sort of second exposure?' muttered David, leaning over the tray.

'That's impossible.'

'I know. Look—on the square. Lines. Can you see them? Down and across, like a grid. Like—'

'Bars!' yelled Frankie. 'It's a barred window—and those two pale streaks poking through. Are they ... arms ...?'

Frankie and David leaned closer, leaving Alice and Michael facing one another across the bench.

44

'Look now! That shadowy blob right in the middle of the grid. It's a—'

Suddenly David and Frankie jerked back as though they had been hit.

'—It's a face...'

Alice nodded. 'She's here,' she said.

The woman stared out through the iron grille, her expression fierce with urgency. Her mouth was open in a shout. Her eyes looked huge and dark in a face mottled with dirt and bruises. Her head was roughly shaved. She had thrust her fists out through the grille and, as the image grew stronger, they could all see that her hands had been damaged in some way. The fingers were swollen and bleeding.

For a few seconds, the image was clear in every detail, then it began to darken and fade. Quickly, David lifted the print from the developing fluid and slid it into the fixative tray, but the image would not stay.

'Now, see, if that was just an ordinary exposure, the fixative would have stopped it from fading. I can't explain it,' muttered David.

'Yeah, but they can,' said Frankie,

45

jerking her head at Alice and Michael.

David shook his head. 'If I don't know what's happening, they won't.'

'It's not about developing film, Davey.' Frankie raised her eyebrows at Alice. 'Is it?'

'No,' sighed Alice. 'I saw that woman at the castle on Tuesday night.'

'What?' said David. 'Don't be stupid. It's a faulty film or something—'

'That's why you passed out, right?' guessed Frankie.

'I didn't see anybody ...' said David.

'And what about you, Michael?' asked Frankie.

Michael swallowed nervously. 'I didn't see anything, but—I—I didn't like it there. I felt as though someone had ... noticed us. Someone not very nice.'

'That's what I felt!' said Alice. 'It was like a door opening. Then something came through. Something really evil ...'

'You mean that woman was bad?' asked Frankie.

'No ...' Alice frowned, thinking back. 'No. I don't think she was the bad one. It was something ... someone else.'

'All right,' sighed David. 'If we must

46

talk about a woman who wasn't there, I'd say she looked pretty evil, if you mean the one in the print—and she was behind bars. She must have done something wrong...'

'Oh, sure,' mocked Frankie.

'Look, you don't get put in prison for nothing.'

Frankie laughed. 'What do they teach you people in history class? Davey, you don't have to be right to put a person in prison, you only have to be stronger than them. What do you think, Alice? Was she good, or bad?'

'Hang on a minute,' said David. 'This woman. Even if she was there, somehow, there are no windows or bars at the ruins. Where did they come from?'

'The past.' Alice spoke without thinking, but as soon as the words were out of her mouth, she knew they were true. 'She came from the past. She was a prisoner in the castle before it was knocked down.'

'Rubbish!' snorted David.

'Have you got a better idea?' asked Frankie.

'Yes! I think we should investigate this

properly, not make up crazy answers.'

'So, what do we do?' asked Alice.

For once, David and Frankie were in complete agreement.

'We go back,' they said.

CHAPTER FIVE

Martha was singing. She was singing a high-pitched, wordless song to make them think she was awake. For days and nights they had been marching her back and forth in the little cell, refusing to let her sleep. After a while the cold, wet flagstones and the sour-smelling straw seemed as welcoming as her own sweet bed, but, every time she tried to lie down, they would slap her face and stamp on her hands until she struggled to her feet. Then the walking would begin again.

So, Martha was singing. As long as they could hear the song they let her be. The song frightened them, she could tell. The fools thought she was calling up the worm which pleased her. Martha wanted to laugh. She had hooked her arms

48

through the grille of the door at the start of her song and now her body stayed upright, even though she had left it. They thought she was awake but she had gone beyond sleep. She was tranced. Her crushed hands and cut feet did not matter now. Only one thing mattered. She must endure until the children returned. There had been four of them, two so shadowy they were hardly there at all. The pale little boy, he had shimmered in and out of sight, but the girl with the long black hair had been, once again, as clear as day. Martha knew that the girl was the link. The girl was her one, her only hope.

*   *   *

Martha was waiting for the girl.

CHAPTER SIX

'Alice,' sighed David, straightening up from the task of chaining their bikes together. 'There are people fishing down at the river. Kids playing football ... the station's busy ... What can happen? The sun is shining—'

'It's dark beside the wall, though,' muttered Alice, staring down the slope at the ruins.

'It's not dark, it's ... in shadow.'

'It's dark! It's always dark there.'

'Alice, there's nothing to be scared about.'

'That's all right for you to say. Me and Michael—'

'Yes!' Frankie stabbed her finger at the castle plan she had bought from the tourist information centre. 'There it is! A dungeon, right where you saw the woman. Come on.'

She set off down the slope without a backward glance.

'Don't you just hate the way she does that?' said David, glowering after Frankie.

'What?'

'Just marches off thinking we'll all follow.' David shoved his hands in his pockets, kicked at a stone, then, with a rueful grin and a shrug of his shoulders, he set off after Frankie.

Alice frowned at the castle ruins,

trying to shake off the awful feeling that something was waiting for her there.

'Do you want to?' asked Michael.

'What?'

'Follow David following Frankie.'

Alice grinned briefly, then picked up the stone David had kicked and began chipping at the wall. 'I hope I'm right, Michael. I wish I could be sure she's not the bad one. What do you think?'

'The woman? In the photograph she looked—trapped. And she's scared because the one who's got her, he's—cruel. She doesn't know what he'll do next, how far he'll go.'

Michael's face had tightened up. His hand slid into his pocket and pulled out his keys. 'I'd like to help her. I—know how she feels,' he whispered, running the keys through his fingers.

'Is that why you said "dad" on Tuesday night, when it started?' asked Alice, carefully.

Michael nodded. 'It felt like my dad was there. I thought he must have followed me to the castle.' Suddenly, Michael put his keys away and lifted his head. 'My dad, he's not that bad though.

51

It's just, he can be a bit much. He needs to be in charge, especially since he lost his job.'

'But, Michael, the way he treats you. Sometimes it's like he hates you—'

'He's not bad.' Michael gazed at Alice. His eyes were bright. 'He's not.'

Alice crossed her fingers behind her back. 'Course he's not bad. He's very . . .' she struggled to find something good to say about Michael's dad. '. . . clean.'

Michael gave a surprised yelp of a laugh and, try as she might, Alice could not stop the giggles from spluttering out.

'Clean . . . ?' gasped Michael, and they began to stagger down the steep path, clinging together and howling with laughter.

*   *   *

The fear returned as they cut across the grass to the ruins. Alice had to force herself to step into the chilly shadow of the wall. She refused to look at breakneck stairs, concentrating instead on watching Frankie pace out imaginary walls.

52

'OK,' said Frankie, coming to a halt. She frowned at the plan then gouged a hole in the grass with the heel of her Doc Marten to mark the spot. 'There. That's where the door was, just about. That's the only place she could have been standing. This dungeon didn't have a window. No point. It was right down in the centre of the castle. I reckon she was looking out through a kind of hole in the door, see? OK everyone move to where you were on Tuesday.'

Reluctantly, Alice moved into position.

'Great! OK now, Alice, can you—'

'—turn about.'

Alice jumped. In mid-sentence, Frankie's American drawl had changed to a lilting local accent. The voice was different too. Deeper. Older. Alice squeezed her eyes shut. She took a breath.

'Say that again, Frankie.'

'Turn about, child,' the voice ordered.

'Frankie!'

'Turn…'

Alice willed herself to stay still but the ball of her right foot lifted clear of the

53

ground, moved round to the side and came down again. Her left foot followed and slowly she began to shuffle round on the axis of her heels. As she turned, the rough, springy grass underfoot changed to solid stone, the shouts of the footballers faded away and the breeze dropped. Alice began to cry. The sound of her sobs bounced back at her, echoing in her ears.

'David! Michael!' she called. There was no reply. Alice came to a stop and stretched out her hands but no one clasped them. Her friends had gone.

Alice did not want to see where she was. She kept her eyes closed and covered her mouth with her hands to stifle the crying. This had to be some sort of illusion. The only thing to do was to keep still and quiet and wait for it to end. As she waited, Alice became aware of someone breathing just in front of her. She began to tremble. The trembling grew worse and worse, until she was shaking so much, the zip fasteners on her jacket started to rattle.

'Now, look at you, child,' scolded the voice. 'Shivering with cold in those thin coverings. You need a good warm plaid around you at this time of year.'

The woman sounded so much like her mum that Alice forgot all about keeping quiet. 'It's a thermal jacket!' she protested, opening her eyes. The woman from the photograph looked back at her. The bruised and dirty face, the damaged hands, the shaven head were all still there but now the lips were cracked and bleeding and the eyes stared out from deep sockets. Alice gasped and closed her eyes again as a mixture of pity and disgust swept through her.

'You're worse,' she blurted. 'I mean ...'

Amazingly, there was a laugh in the voice. 'It is none of my doing, child.'

There was a pause, as though the woman was waiting for Alice to reply, but she stayed silent, eyes closed.

'I am called Martha,' said the woman. 'And you?'

'Alice. And I don't want to be here.'

'Nor I!' said Martha. 'But only one of us must stay.'

Alice opened her eyes. 'You mean I can go back to my friends? When?'

'When we have talked.'

'What do you want?'

'I need to ask you something. I am trapped within these solid walls, yet behind you I see a ruined castle, with sky above and grass for a floor. Tell me, Alice. Are you ...' Martha hesitated. When she spoke again, her voice trembled. 'Are you from the future?'

'No!' yelled Alice, glaring at Martha. 'You are from the past!'

Martha's face lit up with a relieved smile. 'As you wish. I am from the past.'

'Then you—' Alice bit down on her lip to stop it from wobbling. '—you must be a ghost.'

Martha gave a very unghostly laugh. 'Not yet, child.'

'But, how ...?'

'How do our times meet? Alice, we live in The Borderlands. Some call them The Debatable Lands. Borders, you see, are always special. Borders mark the edge of things, and sometimes edges will fray.'

'Like—a piece of cloth?'

'Yes. The edge frays and the pattern unravels, just a little. And some people— only a few—can look through the gaps in the weave, to another time. I found my first gap down by the river there, when I was about your age. I saw a long, sleek ship coming upriver from the sea. It had a curving prow, topped with the head of a beast, and its sides were studded with round shields. I turned to my companions to point out the ship, but they had disappeared.'

'That's just what happened to me! One minute Michael and Frankie and David were all there, the next I was on my own. Weren't you afraid, when it happened to you?'

'Yes. Even now, it frightens me a little. But the pattern will not harm us, Alice. How can it? We are all part of it.'

'Yes, but if we're all part of it, then why can't all my friends see it? Why only me—and Michael a bit?'

Martha thought for a moment, closing her eyes and resting her forehead against the grille. 'I do not know the whole answer, but I will try. Michael is the pale child, yes? I think he is sensitive to others, but no more. He could feel the gap in the pattern only because you were there. He picked it up from you, Alice.

57

As for you …' Martha paused again, searching for the right words. 'It seems to me that most folk are sure of their place in the pattern but, sometimes, for a while, a person does not fit their place very well. You are at a time of great change, Alice. You are changing from a girl to a woman.'

Alice blushed. 'But every girl does that—'

'True, but there is something more with you. I think you are perhaps looking for your place in the pattern?'

Alice thought of the cuckoo days and nodded.

'So, perhaps only those who look hard enough can see the gaps.'

'Yes, but—'

'Enough!' Martha straightened up. The kindness had left her eyes. Her face, framed by the grid, looked hard and tired. 'Enough of this. I told you, I do not know the whole answer—and I am running out of time! You must do—' Martha paused, then tried again. 'I need you to—I ask you to do something for me.'

'What?' muttered Alice.

'The hill by the river, two miles from here. Is it still called Worm Hill? Do you know it?'

'Ye-es.'

'Good. I want you to go there—'

'But—'

'And climb the East side. You must head for the rock outcrop that looks like the head of a dragon—'

'Just a minute—'

'When you reach the outcrop—'

Alice took a deep breath. 'Wait! On Tuesday, I felt something really—evil. Are you . . . ?'

'Evil? What do you think?'

Alice studied Martha's battered face. 'No. The evil was there, though. I felt it.'

Martha nodded grimly. 'I think my jailer must have been nearby. Sir Robert, Lord of the East March.'

'But you could be fooling me. David says you must have done something bad to be in prison. So, I can't do what you want until I know why you're here.'

Martha straightened up. Her eyes flashed as she pushed her face up against the grid. Alice flinched but stood her ground.

59

Martha sighed. 'Very well. I will tell you.'

CHAPTER SEVEN

Alice came awake in terror, thinking that she was falling from a great height. Her body jerked as she braced herself for the impact—but she was already on the ground. She was lying on the grass beside break-neck stairs.

'She's back,' said Frankie, studying her with interest. 'What happened?'

'Shut up, Frankie,' said David. 'Give her time to come round.'

'Are you all right?' whispered Michael, hovering anxiously.

Alice nodded, which was a mistake. She turned onto her side and was very sick into the grass.

'Oh, yuck!' yelled Frankie, dancing away. 'Oh, gross!'

Without a word, David took out a handkerchief and wiped her mouth. He pressed his hand against her forehead and the dizziness stopped.

60

'Better,' Alice said, gratefully, remembering why she liked him so much. She sat up. 'I want to get away from here.'

Between them, David and Michael helped her to her feet and walked her down the slope to the river. Frankie jogged alongside, chattering all the while.

'Alice, that was the weirdest thing! Do you know what you did? OK I'll tell you what you did. You kind of shuffled round on the spot until you were looking right at me, OK? But you weren't looking at me at all! It was weird! Then you shouted all our names, stuck out your hands and keeled over. Alice, I have to tell you, that was one spectacular faint. You didn't even fold up on the way down! And—'

'Frankie,' warned David.

'OK!' grumbled Frankie, flinging herself onto the riverbank.

David rinsed his handkerchief in the river and cleaned Alice up, frowning with concentration. 'There,' he said, finally. 'Now, can you tell us what happened?'

'You're not going to believe this, David. I've been talking to her. The woman we saw in the print.'

David's eyebrows barely flickered. 'Go on,' he said.

Alice blew her fringe out of her eyes and looked up at the sky. 'The first thing is, she's from the past.'

'Aw!' Frankie thumped the bank with her fist. 'How come I didn't get to talk with her?'

'How far in the past?' asked David.

Alice hesitated. 'She talked about the Stuart King. When would that be?'

'King Stewart?' said Frankie. 'Wasn't he the one who burned the cakes?'

'James was a Stuart,' said Michael. 'That was, um, the end of the sixteenth century, I think.'

'Wow!' said Frankie, and she lapsed into silence.

'Was I right about her?' asked Michael.

'I think so. There was this man called Sir Robert. He was Lord of the East Marches and he owned everything around here. He was the bad one, by the sound of it, not her.'

'But she was the one in prison,' said David, doggedly.

'Only because he put her there.'

'Why?'

'For being a witch. But Martha—that's her name—she says she's one of the cunning folk, not a witch. She helps babies to be born and makes sick people better with herbs and things. She learned it all from her mother. She's done it for years. That's how she met James, Sir Robert's son. He came to see her for a cure for his dreadful headaches and she asked him a lot of questions and then told him it was his father giving him the headaches because he was so dom ... domin...'

'Domineering,' said Michael. 'That means really bossy.'

'After that, James came to see her a lot, to talk. He said it helped. They got very close and after a while Martha found out she was going to have his baby.'

'Uh-oh,' said Frankie. 'Trouble.'

'Well, there wouldn't have been trouble if Martha had done what she was supposed to. She was supposed to keep

63

quiet, marry somebody from the village and hand the child over to the castle when it was born. It was the accepted thing to do, but Martha wouldn't even think about it. She stayed single and, when her daughter was born, she wouldn't let her go.'

'Yeah, I can see why,' said Frankie. 'I mean, any mom would hate to let her kid live in a castle surrounded by money and jewels and—'

'Frankie!' said David.

'You've got the wrong idea about the castle. Martha said it was a cold, hard place with no love in it. She said,' Alice screwed up her eyes, trying to remember the exact words. 'She said if a child is to grow properly it must be surrounded with love. Love is the most important thing for a child.'

'Yeah, but the kid would have had her dad to look out for her.'

'No. Martha said he was too damaged to really love anyone, even his own daughter.' Alice stopped to think about what she had just said and suddenly started to cry. David handed over another handkerchief and she sank her face into the clean cotton.

'Two hankies?' marvelled Frankie. 'The guy's a walking laundry. What is it with you British? When you're not passing out, you're crying.'

'Do you mind?' said David, stiffly. 'Alice's real dad left before she was born. She's never met him.'

'Oh. Sorry.' Frankie slumped on the riverbank again. 'I just want some action,' she grumbled into the grass. 'Hey, let's go back up there and—'

'Be quiet!' said Michael. They all stared at him in amazement and he ducked his head. 'Sorry,' he muttered. 'I'd like to know what happened, that's all.'

'OK,' said Alice, wiping her eyes. 'Well, Sir Robert was furious, especially when James tried to stand up to him about it all.'

'He did?' asked Michael. 'He stood up to his dad?'

'Yes, but he soon gave in.'

'Oh.' Michael looked down at his hands.

'Martha knew he would. She said it wasn't James's fault, his father had

65

trained him too well. Anyway, she stayed put for a while, bringing up her daughter. She was beginning to think Sir Robert was going to leave her alone. Then word came from the castle that the old man had gone to get the papers which would let him try her as a witch.'

David sat up straight and folded his arms. 'On what evidence?' he demanded. 'You have to have evidence.'

'He had a signed statement, from James, saying that Martha had used potions and spells to bewitch him and turn him against his father.'

'What?' shrieked Frankie. 'Talk about spineless!'

Michael got up and walked stiffly to the water's edge. He picked up a handful of stones and started skimming them across the surface, one after the other.

'So, come on,' said Frankie. 'What'd she do?'

'When she heard about Sir Robert's plans for her, Martha knew he meant to kill her mother and the child too, if he could. She told me that even sensible people go a little crazy when there's a witch scare. She knew they all believed

66

that witches ran in families and not many would move to help a witch child.'

'He'd kill a little baby?' said David.

Alice nodded. 'First she had to get rid of all her herbs and medicines and she had to hide her mother and the baby before Sir Robert got back with the papers. She had a place all ready, up on Worm Hill.'

Alice pointed upriver to the strange, straight-sided hill which rose so suddenly out of the flat coastal plain.

'Martha's village was at the bottom of the hill on the East side. She told me about a cave, near the top. She hid everything there, the herbs, her winter stores, the goats, everything.'

'That was a bit close to home, wasn't it?' asked Frankie.

'Ah, but it's not called Worm Hill for nothing,' said Alice. 'There are lots of old stories about that hill. It's supposed to have been made by a great worm.'

' 'Scuse me?'

'Dragon to you, Frankie. It was a huge, smoke-breathing monster which came out of the river one winter and ate everything in sight—crops, animals, people—until it was full. Then it coiled around and around until it had made a great pile of rock. It burrowed into the middle of the hill and went to sleep. It's supposed to be in there still, the worm. The stories say it'll come out again one day, when it's hungry.'

Frankie peered at Worm Hill. 'It looks like a volcanic plug to me, like the one they built the castle on in Edinburgh. I know about these things, see, with my dad being a geophysicist.'

'We knew that too,' said David. 'About the volcanic plug.'

'But they didn't know that in Martha's village,' said Alice. 'They believed the stories. That's why Martha was pretty sure no one would go near the cave. She said she'd been ... preparing the ground, that was it. Just in case.'

'What did she mean by that?'

'I don't know, I didn't ask.' Alice stopped and rubbed her hand over her face. She was getting to the difficult bit.

'One night, when the cave was all ready, she and her mother climbed the hill. On the way up, she carried her daughter in her arms. She came back

68

down alone. A few days later, Martha was arrested.'

Alice looked out over the river. Six swans glided past in formation, leaving a fan of triangular wakes behind them. Gulls soared and swooped under the arches of the Royal Border Bridge and a racing canoe sliced through the brown water, heading for the harbour mouth. She watched the canoe until the bridge hid it from view.

'It's awful, what they've been doing to her,' she gulped. 'They won't let her sleep. If she tries to lie down, they beat her until she gets up again.'

'Why?'

'To make her tell them where her daughter is. She looks dreadful, even worse than in the print.'

'Did she say why they shaved her head?' asked Michael.

'They said they were looking for the witch's mark, but Martha says they could have picked on any mole or spot. They didn't need to cut off her hair.'

'That's horrible,' said Frankie, turning to look back at the castle ruin.

'The thing is, she wants me to do

69

something for her.'

'I'll help,' said Michael promptly, turning his back on the river and staring up at the castle.

'Me, too,' said Frankie.

David was silent. They all turned to look.

'But what does she want?' he asked.

'She wants us to find out what happened to her daughter. Oh, David, she knows she's going to die and she's being so brave about it. She doesn't want to die, but she says it won't be so bad if she knows she managed to keep her daughter safe.'

'But, even if we do find out what happened, how are you going to tell Martha?' asked David.

Alice looked up at the shadowy ruins and shivered. 'I'm going to have to go back and talk to her again.'

'Oh, no you're not. Look at the state you were in this time. Anyway, what difference would it make? We're talking about something which happened nearly five centuries ago. It's all over!'

'It's not in the past for Martha,' said Alice, quietly. 'It's happening right now.'

'If it happened at all.' David climbed to his feet and carefully brushed down the knees of his jeans.

'Martha wants me to go to the cave.'

'Yeah!' shouted Frankie. 'Let's all go. We might find something really gruesome—like two skeletons.'

David turned his back on Frankie and began to walk up the hill.

'I know where we should go,' said Michael, quietly. 'We should go to the archivist's office.'

David stopped and waited for Michael to catch up. 'It's in the Council House. They've got all the local history records there, and the archivist is really nice. She helped me with my project on the town walls. I'm sure she'll help us find out about Martha.'

'That's the first sensible idea I've heard all afternoon,' said David, looking relieved. 'Facts and figures, that's what we need. We can find out once and for all whether there's any truth in this.'

'I'll go,' offered Frankie as they reached the top of the hill. 'Dad hasn't got round to thinking about school for me yet, and I'm not going to push it. I can go to the Council House first thing Monday, then I'll meet you guys at the school gates to tell you what I find out. OK?'

'Well, all right,' said David, doubtfully, bending to unchain their bikes. 'But, Frankie, if you're meeting us at the school can you, you know, think about the clothes?'

Frankie grinned. 'Davey, I promise I will choose my outfit very carefully, just for you.'

David looked surprised. 'Really? You will?'

'Sure thing!' called Frankie, cycling off.

'I'd better go too,' said Michael. 'My dad...'

'Take care,' called Alice.

'Will you be all right?' asked David, adjusting his bicycle clips.

'Yes. I'll be fine.'

David scuffed at the ground with the toe of his shoe.

'What's it like, Alice? Being in a different time?'

'I don't know about actually being

72

there. It feels more like wearing a virtual reality helmet. I mean, I'm standing there. I can hear and I can see, but it's not complete.'

'What do you mean?'

'It's like I'm in a sort of bubble. I can't smell anything. And I don't think I'd be able to touch anything either, if I tried.'

David grimaced. 'I'd hate it. I think I'd go mad if it was happening to me. I don't like things that can't be explained.'

'I know.'

'Oh, well, maybe by Monday afternoon we'll have everything sorted out.'

Alice nodded and smiled as she waved David off, but she knew this was not going to end at the Council House. This was going to end at the top of break-neck stairs. In her dreams she crouched on the top slab of stone and the wet, black footprints were only seven steps away.

CHAPTER EIGHT

On Monday, the footprints were two
steps nearer and Alice were through the
school day on automatic pilot. On
Saturday, the footprints would reach
her, and then what?

As she dragged across the yard after
the last bell, Alice heard a commotion at
the school gates. A crowd was gathering
on the pavement, clapping and cheering.
Alice moved up to the outer edge of the
crowd but all she could see was the odd
flash of fluorescent pink between the
ranks of black uniforms. Alice pushed
her way in, listening to the scraps of
conversation floating from the front.

'What a sight! I don't know how she
dares...'

'She must be selling something. Are
you selling something?'

'She's good on those blades, though.'

'Frankie!' gasped Alice, forcing her
way through. 'It's got to be Frankie.'
Instantly, she felt her spirits lift. By the
time she reached the front, there was a

broad smile on her face.

'Hey, Alice!' yelled Frankie. 'I got Michael here. Two down, one to go.' She went into a dazzling spin and the crowd cheered again.

'David's going to love this,' whispered Michael when Alice sat down on the wall beside him.

'But isn't she something?' laughed Alice, studying Frankie's outfit. The top was pink, to match the streaks she had put in her hair. The tights were yellow, to match the banana earrings. The emerald green tutu didn't match anything as far as Alice could see.

'Frankie told the archivist she had a friend in America who thought Martha might be an ancestor,' said Michael. 'The archivist said to come back at four when she'd had a chance to look into it.'

'So we're all going?'

'Looks like it.'

'Hey, Davey! Over here!' yelled Frankie. 'See?' she fluffed up the tutu. 'Just for you.'

The crowd whistled and hooted. 'Oooh! Just for you Davey!'

David turned on his heel and walked

away.

'Coming through! Coming through!' sang Frankie, parting the crowd and speeding off after him.

'Oh, no,' groaned Michael. 'Not again.'

Alice and Michael grabbed their bags and hurried to catch up.

Frankie was buzzing around David like a mosquito. 'OK, so you hate the outfit, right? Is that it? Is that it, Davey? Or maybe I smell. Do I? Do I smell or something?' She flew past his face, flicking his tie out of his coat on the way.

'Leave me alone!' shouted David. He tried to push Frankie away, but she zipped out of reach.

'C'mon, Davey. You can tell me.'

'You look so stupid! I can't believe your dad lets you go out dressed like that.'

'He's cool.'

'Your mum, then.'

Frankie stumbled and nearly fell. She said nothing.

'Oh!' crowed David. 'Hit something there, didn't I? At least someone in your family's got taste—'

'Mom's not here,' cut in Frankie.

'I'll bet she's not here! Anyone'd need a break from living with you once in a while—'

'She's dead!'

David came to a stop and stared at Frankie with a horrified look on his face.

'She's dead. And I don't like talking about it. And neither does my dad. So don't you dare talk to him about it, or tell anyone else. And don't you ever mention this again.'

'I won't. I won't.' David put out his hand but Frankie turned and skated away.

David covered his eyes with his hand. 'I feel dreadful,' he said.

'David, you weren't to know,' said Alice. 'But you were trying to get at her again, weren't you?'

'Yes, but she was getting at me!'

'You haven't exactly made her feel welcome here.'

David sighed. 'She's just so—over the top, you know? She brings out the worst in me. I only have to see her and I can feel myself turning into Uncle Andrew!'

Alice giggled. David's uncle was a

batchelor, fussy and set in his ways. He lived and worked on the farm and he followed a weekly routine which never varied because he hated change of any sort.

'I think you bring out the worst in Frankie, too,' she said. 'I think she sees you being all disapproving and it makes her even more over the top.'

Frankie had stopped a little way up the road and was moodily practising turns around a drain cover. David watched her. 'That must be the worst thing in the world, your mum dying. The worst thing ... No wonder she acts crazy.'

'Oh, David, I don't think ... I mean, I think Frankie's just like that anyway—'

David wasn't listening. 'Well, I'm going to be much more patient from now on,' he said, still watching Frankie. 'She deserves a bit of patience, and if that means me walking along the street with her looking like a mad ballerina, then that's what I'll do.'

David hurried up to Frankie and they headed along the road to the Council House together.

'How long do you give it?' asked Alice.

Michael laughed with her, but the look of relief on his face was unmistakable.

* * *

'Hello, Frankie! Come in. And the rest of you. My name's Jane. Come and see what I've found out for you.'

They filed into the archivist's office, Frankie in her socks with her roller boots tied over one shoulder. Jane led them to a table at the far end of the room. Alice looked sideways at the leather-bound books strewn across the table and swallowed nervously. Was Martha real, or not? Alice couldn't decide which news would be worse.

'I've been through everything. Quarter Sessions Records, Sheriff's Court Records, the lot. Nothing. Except here.' Jane gently opened the book nearest to her. Alice gripped the edge of the table and stared at the faded script which covered the thick, yellowed pages. 'These are Sir Robert's own family records and finances. He did apply to the

79

Privy Council for a commission to try and burn a witch, in 1597, and the woman he arrested was called Martha.'

David sat down rather suddenly and stared at Alice. She smiled weakly, torn between relief that she was not mad and sadness for poor, real Martha.

'Does it say anything else?' asked Michael.

'Oh, yes. You're lucky. There's quite a lot of detail here, which is unusual. There was a witch-hunting craze at that time and a lot of landowners and officials used it to get rid of awkward people on the quiet.'

'That's not right!' said David.

'No, but that's how it was. Anyone with a bit of power could apply for a Privy Council commission. Add to that all that people who accused their neighbours of being witches just because they didn't like them and you begin to realize that a lot of women were burned to death for no reason at all.'

Alice took a shaky breath. 'What— what happened to her?'

'Well, she was taken to the castle and charged with bewitching Sir Robert's son, but she wouldn't confess. They seemed very keen to know the whereabouts of her daughter but she wouldn't tell them that either.'

'So they never found out where her little girl was?' said Frankie.

'No.'

Alice thought about telling Martha that her daughter was safe. She could just imagine how the bruised and battered face would light up with pleasure, and with pride. Alice smiled. She looked round at the others and they were smiling too. Martha had done it!

'Yes, she must have been a tough woman,' said Jane, still scanning the book. 'Mind you, she got off lightly compared to some. They did dreadful things to suspected witches to make them talk. Hot irons, thumbscrews, boots to crush the feet ...' Jane shuddered. 'No wonder most of them confessed. All they did to Martha was walk her to keep her awake, nothing else. I wonder whether someone at the castle was trying to make it easier for her?'

'James,' breathed Michael.

'Still, she did well not to confess to

anything. After a few days without sleep, most people start to rave and ramble and say things they don't mean. Martha actually did start talking to herself, according to this. Of course the writer claimed she was talking to a familiar.'

'A familiar?' said Frankie. 'What's that?'

'A familiar was a witch's helper, supposedly sent from the Devil. It could be anything. An animal, an insect ... In Martha's case they said it was an invisible child, called Alice.'

The shock knocked Alice back in her chair. 'That's my name,' she gasped.

'That's nice, dear,' murmured Jane.

Alice and David stared at one another. 'But, that means the times really did meet!' said David.

Jane looked up from the book. 'Sorry?'

'Nothing,' Alice muttered, slumping against the table.

'Now this is interesting,' said Jane, tapping the page with her finger. 'There seems to have been a bit of a panic when they burned her. It was a public execution, so there was a crowd and, apparently, there was some sort of mass hallucination. Ridiculous as it sounds, they all thought they saw a—well, I'll read it to you.

' "The witch was put to the stake and at this time there came a great roaring and a dreadful worm, called up by the witch, did fly through the very wall of the castle. The worm did fly at great speed over the heads of the people and did light up the air with its burning eyes." '

Jane looked up. 'A worm is a—'

'—Dragon,' said Michael, getting up and walking to the window. Worm Hill loomed on the sky-line.

'When did they burn her?' asked Alice. 'What was the date?'

'Um ...' Jane looked back to the start of the entry. 'It was the afternoon of the 27th of September, 1597. Now, isn't that strange? It's the anniversary of the execution on—'

'—Saturday,' said Alice. Her stomach felt as though it was packed with chips of ice. 'It's this Saturday.'

Jane left them to read on through the ledger. David, careful David, wanted to make sure that Sir Robert never did find

Martha's child. The handwriting in the ledger was elaborate, with s's that looked like f's, and the spelling was terrible, but they kept ploughing through and their hard work was rewarded. A few months on, the ledger recorded the death of Sir Robert in a fall from a bolting horse.

* * *

'Couldn't have happened to a nicer guy,' said Frankie as they ran down the steps of the Council House and into the street. She shivered in the cold East wind as she bent to clip on her roller boots. 'How do you guys stand this weather?'

'This is good for September. Wait until there's snow in that wind,' said David, grimly.

Frankie straightened up and rubbed the chill from her arms. 'I'm for home and a hot tub.'

'Aren't we going to go and tell her, then?' said Alice.

'What? Now?' asked Michael.

'You wouldn't ask that if you'd seen her that second time, Michael. I can't let her go through another night not knowing about her daughter.'

'All right, why not?' said David. 'But let's all go home first. We can dump our school things, have some tea—'

'—and put some warmer clothes on,' added Frankie.

Alice nodded. 'We can meet at the bench next to the ruin at six o'clock.'

'But ...' Michael hesitated. 'Isn't anyone bothered about, you know, the worm?'

'Meaning ...?' said Frankie.

Michael ducked his head. 'The worm. What if she really can call it up?'

'What? Are you serious?'

'O.K. But they all saw it, at the castle. And how was Martha so sure nobody would go near the cave on Worm Hill? She said that strange thing, remember? About preparing the ground?'

David folded his arms and raised his eyebrows. 'Don't push it, Michael. I'm having enough trouble believing that Alice here can chat to a woman who lived hundreds of years ago.'

'But, the ledger said—'

'There is no worm,' said David, slowly and clearly. 'It is a story. A fairy tale.'

Michael shrugged and looked at the ground. His fingers twisted at the buttons on his coat.

'Good,' said David. 'Then we'll meet at six and get this thing sorted. See, Alice? I told you it might all be over by tonight.'

I wish it could be, thought Alice, as she walked up the hill to her house. She thought about Saturday and the ice churned in her stomach.

CHAPTER NINE

'Oh, you came back! Oh, child, you came back!' Martha began to cry and the sobs shook her body as it dangled from the grille.

Alice stared, speechless with shock. In two days Martha had changed from a person to a skeletal shadow. Her fingers had bloated and blackened so that now they hung from her skinny arms like plums from a twig. Her teeth seemed too big for her mouth and her cheekbones looked sharp enough to cut through skin.

It was too much. Alice had never, in her whole life, been face to face with anything as bad as this. How could she talk to someone who was going to die in five days? Alice began to feel very sorry for herself. Her mouth turned down in a resentful pout.

Martha's crying was over quickly. She took a few shaky breaths, then raised her head and fixed her eyes on Alice.

'Child? You have something to tell me?'

'I'm only eleven, you know!'

'Alice, I am sorry, so sorry to do this to you, but you are my only chance. They have found me guilty of witchcraft. In five days I am to die. This is certain. Alice, my strength is all but gone. Please, tell me, if you know, do I tell them before I die? Do I betray my child?'

The whole thing was so big, so important, Alice did not know where to begin, so she scowled at the floor and said nothing.

When Martha next spoke, her voice had changed. The urgency had gone and she sounded warm and friendly, as though she had all the time in the world.

'I called her Tansy. Do you like that name?'

'Tansy?' Alice raised her head. 'I've never heard it before.'

'It is the name of a plant with beautiful, feathery leaves and flowers like yellow buttons. It is a purifying herb, with a strong, clean smell. Tansy has many uses, and it will thrive in any soil. The name comes from the Greek. It means everlasting.'

Alice smiled. 'That's nice. That's pretty.'

'Yes, I think so too. The last time I saw Tansy, she was wrapped in a shawl the colour of tansy flowers. I had made her a little moppet, of the same yellow wool. She was clutching the doll in her fist and laughing as I left the cave. It makes me glad to think of her now.'

Alice was glad, too, thinking about Tansy. 'Don't worry about the next few days,' she said. 'You don't tell them anything, Martha, not a word.'

'I don't?' Martha straightened up and pulled her shoulders back. Her face seemed to come to life. Her eyes shone. 'I don't!'

'Not a word!' shouted Alice, watching the energy flow into Martha. Their laughter rang out under the low roof.

'So, tell me Alice, what did you find in the cave?'

'We didn't go. We didn't need to. His family documents have survived, you see. It was all in there, your arrest and ... the rest of it. They kept asking and asking about Tansy but you never told them where she was. And here's some more good news. A few months from now, Sir Robert dies. He falls off his horse.'

'Ah. What a pity he did not fall last month. He would have saved us all a lot of trouble.' Martha smiled at Alice. 'It is good to know that I do not give in to him, but ...'

'What?'

'Alice, I would ask one more thing of you. Will you still go to the cave? Will you come back and tell me what you find?'

Alice's heart sank. 'But why?'

'Until you go, there is still a doubt, about Tansy. Sir Robert is a ... practical man. Fearless, too. Worm Hill is like any other piece of land to him. Suppose he guessed where I hid them? Suppose he found them, alone and unprotected in the cave? He would kill them both and ride away and never tell a soul. It is not the sort of deed to record in his family documents, the murder of a woman and a child.'

'Go to the cave? I—I'm not sure,' muttered Alice, remembering Frankie's talk of finding skeletons.

'There is no worm to hurt you, on the hill or in it,' said Martha, misunderstanding Alice's reluctance.

'But, if there's no worm, how were you so sure that people would stay away from the cave?'

'The worm is only there for those who fear it, but fear is a powerful force and it grows very easily. I told you—when I thought I might need the cave, I prepared the ground.'

'How?'

'I pointed out the rock outcrop that looked like the head of a dragon. I reminded them of the old stories. I asked first one passer-by, then another, if that was smoke I could see at the top of the hill. I sang as I gathered herbs and did not put a stop to the rumours that I was calling up the worm.' Martha shrugged. 'The word soon spread. It is easy to grow fear.'

Alice looked at Martha in admiration. 'That was clever.'

'Will you go? I need to know that I will not die for nothing. I need to know that Tansy survived.'

Alice thought of the laughing child wrapped in her tansy-coloured shawl. 'Yes,' she said. 'I'll go.'

*   *   *

They went to the fish and chip shop afterwards to get out of the wind. David guided Alice into the café side of the shop and settled her in a booth while he went to order. She sat quietly, listening to Frankie's chatter and gazing around at the checked plastic tablecloths and the steamed-up windows. A television mumbled high on the wall. Nothing seemed quite real.

'You look wiped out,' said David,

when he came back with four cans of drink and two plates of chips to share. He opened a can and pushed it over to her. 'Here, have a drink of this.'

'These aren't fries,' said Frankie, staring at the plate of fat, pale chips in front of her. 'Fries are golden and crispy and good to eat.'

'Ah, but you're talking about burger bar chips,' said Michael. 'These are fish and chip shop chips.'

Frankie picked up a chip and watched in mock horror as it slowly folded in the middle. 'Flabby fries. How gross.'

Michael giggled. 'Does that mean I can have your share?'

'There you go,' said David, pushing his plate over to Alice.

'No thanks.'

'But, Alice, you love chips!' David shook his head. 'It's really taken it out of you, this business. Just as well it's over.'

'It's not.'

David, Michael and Frankie all did a double-take which, under different circumstances, Alice would have found very funny.

'Say again?' said Frankie.

'It's not over yet,' sighed Alice, and she explained about Tansy and the cave. 'I promised I'd go. Will you come with me?'

'Yes,' said David, fiercely. 'I'll come. And if he did kill them, I'm going to make sure everybody in the Borders knows about it, even if it did happen hundreds of years ago. Nobody should get away with that. It's not right!'

'OK. Let me just run this past you,' said Frankie. 'She's going to die anyway, right? So what if you go to the cave and find two piles of bones? Would you go back and tell her? I wouldn't. She might as well die happy, well, sort of. So, why don't we miss out the cave bit, and you can just tell Martha—'

'No! I can't lie to her. She doesn't deserve that.'

Frankie shrugged. 'Whatever. OK. Count me in.'

Michael pushed the chips away. 'What about the worm?'

'Martha said the worm is only there for those who fear it.'

'Yes, well the worm was there for hundreds of people at the castle—'

93

'Aw, come on, Michael! You know how these things go. You get a crowd of hyped-up people, right? Somebody screams, somebody else runs ... Before you know it, you've got a stampede. Then they've got to find a reason for running like a bunch of spooked cattle, so they choose the best story and they stick to it.'

'Frankie's right,' said David. 'Forget about the worm, Michael. It doesn't exist.'

'When do we go?' asked Frankie.

'Saturday,' said Alice.

'That's cutting it a bit close, isn't it?'

'It has to be Saturday,' said Alice, firmly. 'I don't know why, but it has to be Saturday. Saturday morning.'

'Oh, well,' said Michael with a relieved smile. 'I can't go. You know I can't. I have to play chess with my dad on Saturday mornings.'

'Oh, right!' laughed Frankie. 'And I've got a really important Monopoly game I can't get out of ...' She glanced at the others and saw that they weren't laughing. 'Wait just one minute—are you serious?'

'I don't want to do it. He makes me. Every Saturday morning. He says it encourages logical thinking,' said Michael.

'You can get out of it, though, can't you?'

'You don't know his dad,' said Alice.

'Aw, come on, Michael! You don't fool me. You're using your dad as an excuse because you're too scared to go! Michael. You want to help Martha, don't you?'

'Look, she didn't have to end up at the castle. She could have given in at any time, you know. She put herself there.'

'Uh-huh.' Frankie scowled at Michael. 'You are as bad as that James guy. He was too feeble to stand up to his dad and so are you!'

'I am not!'

'No? Then come to Worm Hill!'

Michael jumped up and ran out of the café.

Frankie turned and looked at Alice and David in wide-eyed surprise. 'Was it something I said?' she asked.

CHAPTER TEN

'You're up early for a Saturday, love.' Alice's mum frowned down at the Open University books scattered across the kitchen table. 'Your dad's taken the boys down to the beach, to give me a chance to get on with this essay.'

'Yes, well, don't worry. I won't stay,' muttered Alice, slamming down the cornflakes packet and heading for the door.

'Oh, look, I didn't mean that, you know I didn't! Here, I've cleared a space for you. Come and eat your cornflakes.'

Alice turned and walked back into the kitchen with a sigh.

'You look as though you could have done with a lie-in,' said her mum, studying her pale face and puffy eyes.

'Didn't sleep well,' said Alice. The dream had been so real. She could still remember the cold, rough feel of the stone under her fingertips and the blustery force of the wind as it whipped her hair across her face. The ground was

96

so far below, it made her head reel every time she looked down, so she had stared at the grey stone slab instead, waiting for the final footprint.

She had crouched there for an age, at the top of break-neck stairs. She should have been ready, but when the print suddenly formed out of nothing, soaking into the dust, it was as shocking as a slap in the face. She had stepped back, her heels tipped over the edge of the slab, her arms shot out—and she had jolted awake clinging to her bed.

'Why so early?'

Alice frowned at her mum.

'I said, why are you up so early on a Saturday?'

'Photography project,' said Alice, bringing her cornflakes to the table. 'Old and New. We're going to climb Worm Hill today.'

'Mmmm. I suppose it is one of the oldest things around here. And you should get some wonderful shots from the top. Make sure you've got your key, Alice. We're taking the twins go-karting later on today.'

'Huh! Just as well I am going out,

isn't it?'

'What do you mean?'

'I mean I'm not part of this family any more, am I?'

'Ouch! Foul, ref!' cried Mrs Mitchell, but Alice only stirred her cornflakes around the bowl. 'Alice, the go-karting is plan B. Plan A, if you had nothing else arranged, was swimming and a meal out.'

'Oh. Sorry.'

'Alice. What's on your mind?'

Alice felt her eyes filling up at the gentle tone of her mother's voice. 'I don't look like part of this family,' she said. 'And sometimes … Sometimes, I don't know whether I belong. Not properly.'

Alice blinked and a tear plopped into her cereal milk. Her mum got up and walked to the side of her chair.

'Come here,' she said and held her tight. 'Of course you belong. We all love you so much, Alice. Never think you don't belong. A family is a living thing, right? Like a—a body. A body is made up of lots of parts and they all look different. Does a—a nose look exactly the same as a mouth? No, but they're both part of that body, aren't they? That body wouldn't be whole without a nose...'

'So, I'm a nose, am I?' said Alice, giggling through her tears.

'Oh, dear. I wish I was clever with words.'

'But you are clever, mum. You could have gone to university. You gave up a lot when you had me, didn't you?'

Mrs Mitchell tilted Alice's head and looked into her eyes. 'You are my daughter. There is nothing—nothing!—better than that. I love you. Your dad loves you. Your horrible brothers love you—'

'Surrounded by love,' said Alice, thinking of what Martha had said. 'Mum? I know dad loves me. But—every time he looks at me, he must think...'

'What?'

'... he must remember he's not my real dad.'

Mrs Mitchell drew back and stared down at Alice. 'Have you really been thinking that? No wonder you've been so sad these last few months. Sweetheart, when your dad looks at you, he sees his own daughter, believe me. He is your real dad. He proves it every day. People can't just call themselves mums or dads. They have to earn the name. Don't you think your dad's earned that name?'

Alice nodded.

'Alice, if I tell you something now, will you promise to keep it between us and never tell the twins?'

Alice nodded again.

'All right. Do you know who it was who wanted another baby? It was me. Your dad just wasn't bothered. He had his daughter and that was enough for him.'

'Really?'

'Really. I'm not saying he doesn't love the boys, Alice. Of course he does, very much, but you've always been the special one for him.'

Alice smiled and blew her nose.

'Tell you what, love. Why don't you do Worm Hill tomorrow? We'll go for a swim, shall we? All of us?'

Alice nearly gave in, but the thought of Martha waiting forced her out of the chair and on to her feet. 'Thanks, mum, but I've got to go. I'm expected.'

As she cycled, Alice tried not to think about what they might find in the cave or what was going to happen to Martha. She was working so hard at not thinking about things, it took a few seconds to register that there were three figures waiting at the turn-off to David's farm. Her spirits rose and a surge of energy put new power into her legs.

'Hey, Michael!' she called, as soon as she was near enough. She slowed the bike and pulled in to the side of the road. 'I'm glad you're here.'

Michael grinned at her. There were two bright spots of colour on his cheeks but his gaze was steady. 'I had to be here,' he said, simply. 'It just took me a while to realize it.'

'What did you say to your dad?'

'I didn't,' said Michael, glancing anxiously along the road to town. 'I climbed out of my bedroom window.'

'Wow, Michael!' said Frankie, giving him an admiring look.

'Um. We're in a ground floor flat.'

'Oh, right.'

101

'Ready?' asked David. 'Shall we go?'

'Hang on. Let me get my breath.' Alice stared inland at the square, dark shape of Worm Hill. The sun was shining but the wind was pushing clouds across the sky and their shadows raced over the side of the hill, making it appear to move as though it was breathing.

'Do you know you can see the hill from just about everywhere round here? I never noticed that until this week.'

'Yeah, it's been on my mind, too,' Frankie admitted.

David glanced at his watch. 'We really should go. Dad's pretty sure old Jamieson's at the cattle auction this morning, but he won't hang around if there's nothing to interest him.'

'Who's this Jamie person?' asked Frankie.

'Worm Hill's on his land,' David explained. 'And he doesn't take kindly to people tramping over his fields.'

'Great,' sighed Frankie. 'So we're going to get shot at by an angry farmer, are we?'

'Don't worry, he'll never spot you in that,' grinned David.

Frankie looked down at her orange top and a delighted smile slowly spread across her face. 'Hey, Davey! You made a joke. Way to go, man! Way to go!'

'All right,' said Alice. 'Let's get started.'

There was still a village at the bottom of Worm Hill. It was a small village; one main street, a post-office shop and a pub. A Saturday morning quiet lay over the whole place. Their bike tyres hissed loudly as they cruised along the empty road.

'Blink and you miss it!' called Frankie, once they had left the village behind.

'Jamieson's farm,' called David, pointing out a sandstone farmhouse on the outskirts of the village. The farm looked deserted too, but they kept riding, following the curve of the road around the base of the hill, until the farm was out of sight.

'Stop here!' shouted Alice, pulling in by a five bar gate. She pointed up at the side of Worm Hill. 'See? There's the worm.'

The rock outcrop did look very much like a dragon. A long, narrow overhang

103

formed the snout and there were two shadowy hollows just where the eyes should be.

'That's where we have to go,' said Alice.

David looked over the gate at the field which stretched to the base of the hill. 'It's rough pasture,' he said. 'We can't do any damage.'

'Are those sheep safe?' asked Frankie, eyeing the flock that was spread across the field.

'Don't worry. They only eat grass.'

They hid their bikes in a dry ditch behind a tree and then climbed over the padlocked gate. Alice felt very small and exposed as they crossed the cropped grass of the field but soon they reached the lower slopes of the hill where the grass and weeds grew taller.

'Hey, are you sure those sheep are safe?' panted Frankie, turning to look behind her as they struggled to climb the steepening slope.

'Don't be stupid,' said David, edging between a huge thistle and a patch of nettles.

'Yeah, but they look like they're

ganging up or something...'

David looked round and stopped. The sheep were no longer spread across the grass. They had come together in a tight bunch.

'Something's scared them,' said David.

'Something ...?' Alice stopped, cleared her throat and attempted a smile. 'Like what?'

Michael scanned the hillside with wide eyes. 'I don't see anything.'

'They're running!'

Frankie pointed down the hill to the sheep. They swerved to the right, stopped, then broke to the left. Wherever they ran, they stayed together, like iron filings drawn to a magnet.

'What is it?' said Alice, gazing around. Her heart was beating very fast and her mouth was suddenly dry.

'There,' said Frankie.

They all saw it at once. Above them and over to the right, something was coming down the hill. It was low to the ground and hidden by the undergrowth, but the tops of the long grasses swayed and bent as it passed. It was moving fast

105

on a curving, twisting path.

'Oh, no!' cried Michael.

The four of them crowded together, watching the snaking, sinuous movement come closer.

'It's heading for the sheep,' said David. 'It'll miss us.'

They waited for the thing to pass but the sheep below changed direction once again, moving directly behind them. Above them, the creature turned too.

'It's coming right for us!'

They turned and began a stumbling run down the hillside, but they were too late. The thing burst out of the long grass, right on top of them. Alice screamed when she saw the lolling pink tongue and the sharp teeth. She covered her head as it lunged past her legs.

'It's a dog!' roared David in disgust. 'It's a stupid sheepdog!'

The black and white collie raced down the last part of the hill, leaving them behind.

'Oh, boy,' said Frankie, collapsing to the ground and examining the thistle scratches on her arms. 'I thought we were gonners.'

Alice wiped the sweat from her top lip and giggled weakly. 'The worm is only there for those—'

'—who fear it,' finished Michael, letting himself fall back against the hillside.

'There are two dogs,' said David pointing out a second collie working the road-side of the field. A long, high whistle carried on the wind and they all looked over to the gate they had climbed earlier.

'Uh-oh,' said Frankie, peering at the figure standing by the gate. 'Is that Jamieson?'

'Yes,' said David. 'Keep still. I don't think he's spotted us.'

'He has now,' muttered Frankie as the farmer turned his head and looked straight at them.

'What do we do?' whispered Michael.

David groaned. 'We'll have to go down.'

'But we can't!' Alice cried. 'We need to reach the cave!'

Suddenly, the farmer whistled for his dogs, still watching the children closely. The dogs left the sheep and came to heel.

'Look, we'd better go, before he sets his dogs to bring us down—'

David stopped as the farmer touched his hand to his cap, turned and climbed into his landrover.

'I don't get it,' he said, as the landrover moved off down the road.

'I do,' said Alice. 'He's letting us go on.'

'Jamieson? Why would he do that? He hates people on his land.'

'I don't care why he's doing it, just so long as we get there. Come on.'

'I don't like this,' muttered David, but he followed the others up the slope.

'Hey, look!' panted Frankie a few minutes later. 'We don't need to fight our way through those thistles any more. There's a track here. It leads straight up to the outcrop.'

Gratefully, Alice and Michael fell into line behind Frankie, but David hung back. 'I don't get this either,' he said. 'How can there be a track here? You need regular traffic to make a track like this and Jamieson never lets anybody climb Worm Hill.'

Michael shrugged. 'Sheep? Rabbits?'

'Too wide. And look, it goes in a dead straight line right from the outcrop to—' he looked down the track, '—to the back of those farm cottages on the edge of the village.'

Frankie looked up then down the track. 'He's got a point. This is seriously weird.'

'Those cottages belong to Jamieson's farm,' said David. 'Oh ...' His eyes widened and he became very still. 'Jamieson. Jamieson ... That name means—used to mean—"son of James", didn't it?'

'So?' said Alice.

'James was the name of Sir Robert's son,' said David.

'Are you saying that guy down there with the flat cap and the dogs is a descendant of...'

'I haven't got time for this!' snapped Alice, pushing past and heading up the track. 'I've got to see the cave and get back to Martha before—' She hurried on without finishing her sentence.

They caught up with her at the end of the track. She was stamping around on the rock platform at the base of the outcrop, nearly crying with frustration.

'There's no cave! There's no cave! What are we going to do?'

CHAPTER ELEVEN

They fanned out along the platform and stared up at the rock face. 'It must be the wrong outcrop,' said Frankie.

'But look,' said Michael, from the far end of the platform. He pointed to a fold in the rock directly ahead of him.

'What?'

Michael walked up to the fold, turned sideways—and disappeared.

They were still gaping when he reappeared, seeming to step out of solid rock. 'There's an opening,' he said. 'You can't see it until you're right in front of it.'

Alice rushed up and kissed Michael on the cheek. 'Your dad doesn't know how lucky he is to have you,' she whispered. Michael blushed and stepped back from the entrance with a bow.

'All right,' said Alice, peering at the

narrow opening. 'Are we ready?'

Wordlessly, David took a torch from his pack and handed it to Alice.

The wind stopped as soon as she slipped between the lips of rock. She shone the torch ahead of her. Again, the narrow tunnel seemed to come to a dead end at a rock wall, but Alice was not going to be fooled twice. She walked up to the wall and found another fold of rock where the tunnel doubled back on itself. She poked her head round the tight bend and shone the torch.

'It gets much wider past here,' she called back, easing round the second bend. 'And it turns and heads up into the hill.'

Alice stopped at the bottom of the sloping passage and waited for the others to come through the turn. They clustered behind her and she shone the torch beam upwards. They could all see that the passage opened up at the top.

'That must be the cave,' she breathed. Now that it came to it, Alice found she did not want to go on. She moved the torch around, pretending an interest in the passage walls.

'Look at that!' said David, still staring up at the entrance to the cave.

'What?' Alice trained the torch up the slope again.

'No, you can't see it now. It was only when you moved the torch away. There's a light up there.'

Alice pointed the beam at the floor. 'You're right! I can still see the walls.' She turned off the torch and they waited, letting their eyes adjust to the gentle light filtering down from above.

Michael sniffed. 'Can you smell that? It's like, um, cough sweets…'

'… Mouthwash?' guessed Frankie.

David sniffed. 'No, it's more like that stuff you put on your chest when you've got a stuffy cold…'

Suddenly, Alice wasn't frightened any more. 'I know what it is,' she said, and she walked up the slope and into the cave.

Alice focused on the light first. The cave was shaped like a wedge of cheese, with a wide floor and two long side walls sloping inwards to meet high above her head. Daylight was leaking in through a chink in the top corner of the wedge and pouring down onto a platform of stones below. The wind sighed around the chink in the roof, but the cave was quiet and still. Specks of dust swirled lazily in the column of light.

'It's a natural chimney,' whispered David, coming up beside her. 'See?' He pointed to the centre of the platform where the stones were blackened and scorched. 'Someone used this as a fireplace, once.'

Alice smiled, imagining the smoke curling out of the hillside. 'Dragon's breath.'

'Look!' Frankie's horrified shriek was loud in the quiet cave. Alice spun on her heel and stared into the shadows where Frankie was pointing.

'What? I can't see.'

'Bodies!' cried Frankie, stumbling backwards. 'Little kids!'

'No ...' Alice fumbled for the torch, clicked it on and trained the beam on the row of dark shapes against the wall. For a moment, they all stared in silence, trying to take in what the beam showed. Then Alice began to laugh.

'The-they're not bodies! They're

113

moppets!'

'They're what?'

'Moppets!' shouted Alice, exultantly. 'Home-made dolls! Isn't it wonderful! Look! There must be fifty of them! This is fantastic!'

'I don't know about fantastic,' said Frankie, doubtfully. 'They look pretty grotty to me, especially the ones down at that end.'

'No, you don't get it, do you?' Alice turned to face them. Tears were streaming down her cheeks but her face was so full of happiness, they found themselves grinning back at her without knowing why.

'Tell us,' said David.

'Tansy had a moppet. Martha made it for her out of yellow wool.' Alice ran to the head of the line of dolls and pointed to a shapeless, grey lump. 'I think this was Tansy's moppet. Or maybe there's nothing left of Tansy's moppet now, but that doesn't matter! It was right here at the start of this line, once. Do you see?'

'... Um...'

Alice danced with impatience and moved along to what was left of the

114

second doll in the line. 'This was Tansy's daughter's moppet. And this,' she pointed to the third doll. 'This was Tansy's grand-daughter's moppet. And this—'

'She survived! Tansy survived!' cried Michael. 'Old Sir Robert didn't find her!'

'And here's the evidence,' said David, walking beside the line of dolls. 'It's like a family tree, stretching all the way from her time into ours ... Of course!' David smacked the palm of his hand to his forehead. 'That explains the track, up the side of the hill from the cottages. Martha's family must still be living down there in the village!'

'But why the moppets?' asked Frankie.

'They're for Martha,' said Alice. 'Tansy came back and left her moppet here for her mum. To remember her. To say thanks. And every doll that's been put here since then, they're all for Martha too.'

'Oh, boy,' marvelled Frankie, squatting to peer at a moppet in the middle of the line. 'And no wonder they're all so grotty. They don't come up here until they're worn out and ready to be replaced.'

They walked up the line together in silence, watching as the torch beam played over each doll in turn. The moppets stared back, with button-eyes of bone and wood and brass and bakelite and, finally, bright new plastic.

'This one's pretty recent,' said David, pointing to the last doll in the line. 'See, it's got a little lycra top and leggings...'

'Mmmm. Lime green,' said Frankie. 'Just my taste.'

'When do you think this one was put here?' asked Michael.

'Today,' said Alice and her voice trembled. 'Someone's been here this morning.'

'How do you know?' asked David.

For answer, Alice flicked the torch beam into the corner next to the moppet. Propped against the wall was a huge bunch of freshly-cut plants with beautiful, feathery leaves and clusters of yellow flowers shaped like buttons. They were giving off a strong, clean scent, like camphor.

Michael sniffed. 'That's what I could

smell, in the tunnel.'

'I know,' smiled Alice. 'That's when I knew it was going to be all right, when I smelled them. They're Tansy flowers.'

On an impulse, Alice reached out, picked one of the flowers and put it in her pocket. 'Come on,' she said. 'Let's go and tell Martha.'

*　　*　　*

It was Michael who spotted the garden. They were cycling back past the little row of farm cottages, when he called out to them to stop.

'Look at that,' he said, pointing to the middle cottage. The garden was packed with flowers, vegetables and herbs, each growing in its own tiny space.

'Over by the wall,' said Michael. 'There's a big clump of them.'

'Tansy flowers,' breathed Frankie. 'This must be their house...'

They were still looking at the plants when the cottage door opened and a little girl came out, cuddling a new moppet. She sat on the step and rocked the doll in her arms, singing to it in a clear, high voice.

'Tansy hides, safe inside,
With the worm to guard her.
Martha dies, Tansy cries,
Moppet to remind her.
Tansy grows, Martha knows,
Alice went and told her.'

The last five words of the rhyme sank into Alice's mind like depth charges and exploded a few seconds later, sending out shock waves that left her gasping. They knew! They knew about her! How could that be? Alice shuddered in the warm sunshine.

'Did you hear that?' whispered David. 'Let's go and talk to her.'

'No!' Alice shook her head.

'But I just want to ask her a few questions. Don't you want to know more?'

Alice stared at the little girl. The girl raised her head and returned the stare then nodded, gravely.

'Don't you?' David asked.

'No,' said Alice and she climbed back onto her bike.

'Wait!'

A young woman stepped out of the doorway and stood beside the little girl. She was wearing a leotard, leggings and one trainer. The other trainer was still clutched in her hand. She pushed a fringe of dark hair out of her eyes and stared at Alice.

'Wait.'

The woman hopped and hobbled down the gravel path, wincing as a sharp stone stabbed through her sock. She stopped at the gate and gripped the top bar, balancing. Her face was tense. 'Alice?' she asked.

Alice hesitated, then nodded reluctantly.

The woman's face softened into a smile. Her eyes shone with tears. 'Aerobics class,' she said, waving the trainer. 'I was just getting ready to go. Five more minutes and I would've missed you ...' Her voice trembled. 'Listen to me, rabbiting on. I'm Hazel. If Martha hadn't saved Tansy all that time ago, I wouldn't be here now. Have— have you been up to the cave?'

Alice gripped the handlebars of her bike and cleared her throat. 'Yes,' she muttered.

Hazel pressed her lips together and gave a series of quick nods. She was still staring at Alice as though she could not quite believe her eyes. 'It's true, then. A dark-haired child from the future did talk to Martha before she died.'

'How do you know that?' Alice asked. Fear made her voice sullen, but Hazel did not seem to mind.

'Martha's mother told Tansy and Tansy passed it on to her own daughter—and so on and so on. When my mum told me, I half-thought you were a fairy tale. I thought Martha's mother might have invented you, just to make Tansy feel better. You know what grandmas are like.'

Alice nodded distractedly, thinking hard. A silence grew and David jumped into it.

'Old Jamieson, the farmer. He usually guards Worm Hill as if it was a gold mine or something, but when he saw us today, he let us go on. It was almost as if he'd been expecting us. I was thinking, Jamieson—son of James—is that Martha's James?'

Hazel nodded. 'Worm Hill has been in their family ever since then. They've kept the cave safe.'

'I thought so,' said David, smiling triumphantly at Alice.

Alice did not notice. She was too busy with her own questions. 'But, how did Martha's mother know—about me?'

Hazel shrugged. 'Alice, there's so much I don't understand about this. I don't even know whether I should be talking to you, when you must be in such a rush to get back to Martha.' She hesitated. 'Will you just tell her we always remember her on this date? Will you send her all our love, and our thanks?'

Alice nodded. 'The cave. It's—lovely.' She gave Hazel a wobbly smile, then pressed down on her pedals and rode away.

CHAPTER TWELVE

Martha sat quietly on the stool as the clean linen was wrapped around her head and tied. Her best plaid rested across her shoulders once more and her good skirt hung loosely at her waist. Martha had not expected to see her own things again.

It had started the night before with whispers and the clink of coins changing hands. The door had swung open and a young man had hurried in, carrying a blanket and a pallet stuffed with fresh straw. He had helped her over to the pallet, covered her with the blanket and hurried out again.

It was clean and soft and warm. It was so wonderful, she had cried, just a little, before she plunged into sleep. She did not move all night.

Then, this morning, they had let the woman in, bringing hot comfrey poultices for her poor hands and clear broth to fill her stomach. And now, the woman again, with a copper of hot water and the clean, dry clothes.

James was doing the best he could.

Martha sighed. Each new comfort was a wonder, after all she had been through, but she would have refused them all if she could have found the strength. Martha knew that every minute of sleep, every mouthful of food would make it more difficult to die, when the time came.

The woman finished tying the headscarf and stepped back. She had been silent throughout but her hands had been gentle with the wash cloth, so Martha smiled gratefully. It was so good to be clean.

Alone once more, Martha settled to wait for Alice. There was not much time left but she knew that Alice would not abandon her. The child had a good heart. And a sweet face. Martha thought her own Tansy might grow to look a little like Alice, given time. Martha lay down on the pallet, closed her eyes and prayed that Tansy would be given the time to grow.

The key rattling in the lock brought her awake. Martha climbed unsteadily to her feet. Two guards hurried in. Without a word, they grabbed Martha by the arms and started to walk her out of the cell.

'Wait!' cried Martha. 'It is not time yet. It cannot be!'

'You must be quiet,' hissed the man.

'No! You are too early. Alice has not come yet. I must talk to Alice first. Let me wait just a little longer. A little longer, please!'

123

The men would not listen. They dragged Martha from her cell and headed for the stairs.

CHAPTER THIRTEEN

When Alice reached the castle, the wind had strengthened. It blustered and pushed at her as she hurried down the hill. It whipped her hair into her face just like the wind in her dream. Alice kept her head down, refusing to look at break-neck stairs.

'Come on!' she shouted to the others. 'We've got to hurry!'

'There's plenty of time,' said David, catching up with her. 'The burning was in the afternoon, the ledger said—'

'I know what the ledger said,' interrupted Alice. 'But all of a sudden, I've got this awful feeling that I'm going to be too late.'

'No, no, no.' David shook his head confidently. 'Hazel knew about you, right? That means you must have got to Martha in time—I mean you will get there—I mean I don't think you can be late ... can you?'

'Shut up, David. And stop pretending you understand what's going on.'

'You're only nervous,' said David, kindly.

'Of course I'm nervous! They're going to burn her. What do I say? Oh, it's all right Martha, there's a cave full of dolls up on Worm Hill. That's going to make her feel a lot better.'

'Yes! It will! She's doing this for Tansy, remember? I'm sure—'

'You can be as sure as you like, David. You don't have to face her.' Alice hurried across to the ruin and, for the third time in a week, took up her position on the grass where the dungeon door used to be.

'You'd better stand in the same places too,' she said. 'Just in case it's important.'

Michael stood behind her, David walked to the bottom of break-neck stairs, and Frankie climbed up the first few steps.

'Good luck,' called Frankie.

Alice took a deep breath, closed her

eyes and reached out to Martha. Nothing happened. Alice tried harder. This time she got a bolt of sheer terror, as sudden and blinding as a lightning flash. It was over in a second but it left her gasping and shaking.

'What's wrong?' called David, moving towards her.

'Get back!' yelled Alice. 'Get back into position! There's not much time.'

Alice pulled the tansy flower from her pocket, closed her eyes and, once again, willed Martha to hear her, but the grass stayed under her feet and the wind roared in her ears.

'It's not going to work!' cried Alice. 'She's too frightened and I can't do it on my own. Oh, what can we do? We're running out of time!'

'Alice,' said Frankie, in a soft, wondering voice which made them turn and look at her. She was still standing on break-neck stairs, but she had flattened herself against the wall. She was gazing at the bottom step.

'Look,' she said.

Michael hurried to join Frankie and David. Alice followed slowly, horribly certain of what she was going to see. There it was, the footprint, wet and glistening.

David stared at the print in disbelief. His face was bone white. 'That's impossible.' He looked around at the others. 'Isn't it?' His voice was pleading.

Wordlessly, Michael pointed at the second step. Already a damp smudge was beginning to form. David covered his face with his hands.

'It's Martha,' said Alice, her voice shaking with horror. 'Her feet are wet, see, because the floor of that dungeon is running with water. They must be taking her out early. What do we do? They're taking her out to die!'

'Lemme down!' cried Frankie, close to panic. She launched herself from the stairs, just as the third footprint began to form.

Alice shook her fists at the footprints. 'I can't do this, Martha! I can't follow you up there! Don't you know about me and heights? Don't you know I'll fall?'

The fourth step began to darken. Martha was leaving her behind.

'All right! I'm coming.'

Alice took the stairs in a rush. She managed to get to the ninth step before the stone beneath her feet began to rock. She fell forward, bruising her knees. The stairs lurched as though they were trying to throw her off and the sky wheeled around her head.

It was much, much worse than the dream. At least, in the dream, she made it to the top. At least she didn't give up with so many steps still to climb. Alice closed her eyes and rested her head on the steps, pressing her cheek against the cold stone.

'You dropped this,' said a voice beside her. Alice opened one eye. Michael was bending over her, holding out the tansy flower. She reached out and clutched his hand with the flower in it and felt the dizziness lessen.

'You won't fall,' said Michael. 'I'm going to be right next to you, on the outside, all right?'

Alice opened the other eye. 'All right.'

'Can you stand?' Michael offered his other hand and she grabbed it, allowing him to haul her to her feet.

'Just look at me,' said Michael.

128

'Nowhere else.'

Alice turned and stared into his face. Michael smiled.

'We're going to move now,' he said, very calmly. 'But you've got to tell me Alice, do you want to go up, or down?'

'Up' said Alice, through frozen lips, still staring into his face. The smell of the tansy flower was strong in her nostrils. 'We have to reach the top before the footprints.'

'Here we go, then,' said Michael. 'Lift your foot, Alice.'

Alice really tried, but she could not move. Michael turned slightly to look behind him and she gripped his hands so hard, she made him wince.

'Alice, the footprints are getting nearer. Come on. We can't let Sir Robert win now!'

'Count!' Alice shouted, closing her eyes. 'Count me up them.'

'One, two, three...'

Michael counted and Alice marched to the count and she did not stop until he told her to.

'Brilliant,' he said, squeezing her hands. 'We're here.'

'We are?'

'Right at the top. What now?'

'Just keep hold of me,' said Alice, still with her eyes closed. 'I need to think. OK. I'm in the right place, I know I am. But I'm in the wrong time. I need to get to Martha's time. How do I get to Martha's time ...?'

Alice stopped. An answer was forming in her head. 'Frankie?' she called. 'Can you hear me?'

'Yeah.' Frankie's voice, drifting up from below, seemed awfully far away.

'Frankie, remember your plan of the castle?'

'Yeah ...'

'Can you remember what was at the top of these steps?'

'It was a ... I think it was a sort of inner courtyard. Yeah, that was it.'

'So the steps came up through the floor of the courtyard?'

'Uh-huh.'

'Alice,' said Michael. 'The footprints are nearly at the top.'

'Right.' Keeping her eyes closed, Alice straightened up. She began to chant under her breath, 'The pattern can't hurt me. I am part of the pattern.' As she chanted, she imagined the castle as it was in Martha's time. There was a courtyard spreading out from the stone slab where she stood. There were solid flagstones at her feet, not empty space.

Alice let go of Michael's hand and stepped over the edge of break-neck stairs.

* * *

'Al-ice!'

Michael started the shout, but Martha finished it. Alice gasped and opened her eyes. She was standing on solid ground. It was a courtyard, a small courtyard surrounded by the high walls of the castle. The courtyard was empty but, from somewhere just beyond the walls, Alice could hear the buzzing hum of a large crowd.

'Alice!' Martha's voice was full of terror.

Quickly, Alice turned back to the steps, just in time to see a figure emerge. It was not Martha. It was a man. A guard. Alice froze, but the guard looked straight through her.

A door creaked open across the courtyard. The guard glanced over, raised his hand and turned back to the steps. Reaching down, he grabbed hold of something and pulled. Martha came stumbling up the last few steps and Alice felt weak with relief. She was not too late!

The guard pushed Martha, quite gently, against the wall. 'Wait here,' he said and he hurried past Alice to the door across the courtyard. Left on her own, Martha slumped against the wall, sobbing.

'Alice, please ...' she whispered.

Quickly, Alice moved to stand in front of Martha. 'I'm here,' she said, softly. 'I've been to the cave.'

'Oh, child ...' Martha lifted her head. 'Tell me.'

Alice looked into Martha's face and her throat closed up. Wordlessly, she held out the tansy flower but Martha was adjusting to daylight after her time in the dungeon. She could not see the flower. Still unable to speak, Alice crushed the stem in her outstretched hand.

Martha took a breath. 'Tansy! I smell tansy flowers!'

'They were in the cave, Martha, a whole bunch of them. Tansy survived, Martha. She grew up and had a daughter of her own.'

All the strain left Martha's face. She pushed herself away from the wall and straightened up. 'Then all is well,' she said.

'Oh, Martha! I wish you could have seen it. The cave, it was filled with moppets, stretching from your time into mine! Tansy started it, with the moppet you made for her. She left it in the cave to remember you by and, ever since then—'

'All those mothers and daughters? Even into your time . . . ?' Martha stared at Alice in astonishment.

Alice nodded, laughing through her tears. 'They've never forgotten you, Martha. And they're still living in the village at the bottom of Worm Hill. I saw a little girl there, playing with a new moppet. She was singing a little rhyme all about you.'

'About me? Oh, this is beyond all—'

'Shall I sing it to you? It goes,

133

"Tansy hides, safe inside,
With the worm to guard her.
Martha dies, Tansy cries,
Moppet to remind her.
Tansy grows, Martha knows,
Alice went and told her." '

Martha smiled and her smile was beautiful. 'Thank you, Alice,' she said.

'Quickly! This way!' The shout from behind her made Alice jump. She turned, then stumbled back as the guard hurried past.

'This way, woman,' he said, gripping Martha by the elbow and hurrying her towards the open door. 'The young lord has arranged for someone to be brought to see you, but we must be quick. A few minutes only.'

He beckoned to a shadowy figure waiting in the doorway and suddenly Alice realized who the visitor must be. 'Oh, of course,' she whispered. 'That's how she knew...'

The figure walked out into the courtyard and Martha stopped.

'Mother?'

Martha swayed on her feet and the woman stepped to her side, slipping an arm around her waist. The guard turned his back, scanning the courtyard nervously. Alice crept past him, closer to Martha.

'Mother, it is dangerous for you to be here,' whispered Martha. 'Where have you left Tansy?'

Martha's mother lifted her plaid. A baby girl lay sleeping in the crook of her arm, wrapped in a yellow shawl. Silently, Martha formed her arms into a cradle. Gently, her mother placed Tansy in the cradle, avoiding Martha's damaged hands.

For one still moment, they stood together. Martha gazed down at Tansy. Martha's mother gazed, with the same fierce love, at her own daughter. Martha bent and rested her cheek against the child's face and kissed her forehead.

'James,' said Martha, raising her head to look into her mother's face. 'How did he find you?'

Martha's mother leaned closer and lowered her voice to a whisper. 'He knew we must be hidden somewhere near. When he heard rumours of the worm awakening, he guessed what you had

135

done. He came to the hill alone and followed our tracks up to the cave.' A shadow of worry crossed her face. 'He has kept our secret thus far, but, after the way he betrayed you, I fear to trust him.'

'All will be well,' said Martha. 'I know this.' She turned to Alice and smiled. 'I know. The cave will be safe. Alice has told me.'

Alice nodded eagerly, but Martha's mother only stared unseeingly at the air above Alice's head. 'Another of your visions, Martha?' she asked.

'Alice comes from the future. She lives in a time when this great castle is fallen into ruin.' Martha watched her mother's puzzled stare and smiled. 'Lower, look lower. She is only a child.'

Alice saw the woman's gaze re-focus on her face. The eyes widened. 'Yes. I think I see ... A dark-haired child...'

Alice shivered. It was so strange, feeling as though she was only a shadow. she was glad when Martha's mother gave up the effort and turned back to her daughter.

'Martha ... I cannot stay long...'

'I know.' Martha looked down at

Tansy once more, her face full of a hungry love, then she held out her arms allowed her mother to take the yellow-wrapped bundle.

'Here. Love her as you loved me, and she will be happy.'

When Tansy was hidden under the plaid once more, Martha's mother reached into a pouch at her waist and brought out a small green bottle. She pulled the cork and gently eased the bottle between Martha's swollen fingers. 'To speed you,' she whispered, cupping her hand to Martha's cheek.

'Take her now, mother,' said Martha squeezing her eyes shut.

Abruptly, the woman turned and rushed away through the doorway. The guard was taken by surprise. As he hurried to close the door, Martha swiftly raised the bottle to her lips and drank.

'Child,' she said, turning to Alice. 'You must go back, too. They will take me now.'

'They can't do it!' cried Alice. 'Oh, this is so dreadful!'

'Alice, listen to me. You must not worry. I will feel nothing. The flames will not touch me, for I will be gone.' Martha held up the little bottle. 'Do you understand me?'

Alice nodded. She was crying so much, she could not speak.

Martha's head drooped and she sank to her knees. With a great effort, she raised her head and focused on Alice.

'I thank you, sweet child, with all my heart.'

The guard ran back and dragged Martha to her feet, just as the outer gates of the courtyard grated open.

'Don't stay, Alice,' sighed Martha, in a thick, slurred voice. 'Go back home.' Her head fell forward and she folded to the ground.

With a curse, the guard slung Martha over his shoulder, staggered to the cart which waited at the gates and lowered her onto the straw. Two men pulled the cart out through the gates and the hum of the crowd rose to a roar. Alice was left alone in the courtyard.

She walked as far as the open gates and looked out on a scene both familiar and strange. There was the valley side, but crowds of people were strolling on the grass where the station should stand.

There was the river but no Royal Borders Bridge sweeping across it. Behind her, the castle towered over the landscape.

Alice blinked the tears from her eyes and watched the slow progress of the cart through the crowd. Before she left, she had to be sure of one thing. She made herself watch as Martha's body was lifted from the cart and strapped to the stake. Even from a distance Alice could see that there was no sign of life. What Martha had said was true. She would feel nothing.

As the first flames began to burn, Alice turned and made her way back to the stairs. Her tears had stopped and she felt very tired. She knelt on the top step and concentrated for the first time on the problem of how to get back to her own time. Perhaps if she thought about all the people who were waiting for her there?

Alice pictured David and Michael and Frankie waiting in the ruins. She thought about her mum and dad and the twins waiting for her to come home. As she concentrated, the castle began to fade.

For a few seconds, Alice straddled both times. The flagstones of the courtyard remained, but she could see through them to the grass far below. The Royal Border Bridge shimmered above the river at the same time as a crowd gathered around a great fire. Alice grew afraid. What if she could not get back to her time?

A faint vibration started in the stone under her knees. It turned into a distinct tremble. Alice scrambled to her feet. Below her, the crowd had grown silent. Hundreds of white faces were lifted to the sky as a hissing roar began to fill the air.

Alice raised her head and saw an impossible thing rushing towards her. It came flying over the valley, huge and dark, with its eyes blazing and its long black tail twisting behind.

It seemed to take an age for her lungs to fill with air, for her mouth to open wide, for the scream to come bursting out.

'The worm!' she cried, in a voice which carried across the hillside. 'The worm is coming!'

Below her, black holes appeared in the white faces as the crowd took up her scream. They turned to run, all of them, falling and stumbling and hiding their faces as the worm roared down on the castle.

'I can't die here!' Alice cried. 'I don't belong!' She stared in horrified disbelief at the red and blue streaked side of the approaching beast. And blinked. And looked again.

Suddenly, Alice understood. As the two times blurred together, the worm which a terrified crowd saw flying over a great fire, was also an inter-city train, roaring across the Royal Border Bridge in her own time.

Alice straightened up to watch as the train soared over the heads of the crowd and blasted through the castle wall, headlights blazing. With a thundering rush, it curved and twisted through the air, following an invisible track. The crowd scattered, shrieking in panic and Alice laughed.

'Ha! There's your worm!' She yelled, jumping up and down. 'I hope you all die of fright! I hope—'

Suddenly, there was nothing under her feet. Alice fell and darkness rushed up to meet her. Just before she blacked out, she saw a blue light flashing at the top of the hill.

CHAPTER FOURTEEN

'Alice? Wake up for me, dear. Open your eyes.'

Her ear was hurting. Alice lifted her hand to stop the hurt and touched another hand.

'That's it dear, open your eyes.'

Someone was pinching her earlobe. Alice was irritated. She tried to push the hand away but the pinching continued.

'Come along, Alice.'

'Don't do that,' said Alice, opening her eyes. 'It hurts!'

'Good girl.' The nurse smiled down at her. 'You're in the hospital, Alice—'

'I know that.' Alice raised her head. 'It's the accident and emergency bit. I remember it from when I broke my thumb.' She looked down at herself,

142

lying under the red hospital blanket. 'I haven't broken anything this time, have I?'

The nurse laughed. 'No. Do you remember what happened?'

'... Um ...' Alice decided to play it safe. 'No.'

'You fainted on top of the castle ruins.'

'Did I fall?'

'No. But when you didn't come round, your friends were frightened that you might fall, so they called the ambulance.'

'Oh. Where are they now?'

'We sent them home.' the nurse wrapped a band around Alice's arm. 'I'll just do your blood pressure.' She pressed a button on the machine by the bed and the band filled with air, squeezing her arm.

'OK,' the nurse ripped open the velcro fastening on the band. 'Now—'

The swing doors at the entrance to the unit slammed open with a thud and someone came running down the corridor, gasping and wheezing, skidding into all the side wards on the way.

'Oh, dear,' said the nurse. 'The drunks

143

are in early.'

But it wasn't a drunk. It was her dad. The cubicle curtains ripped open and there he was. His hair was sticking out all around his head like the petals of a flower. He was clutching a half-eaten sandwich and wearing his green, dinosaur-feet slippers.

'Hello, dad,' Alice said, and burst into tears.

*   *   *

They were still laughing about it on Sunday morning. Every now and then a new nurse would peer round the door of the side ward where they had moved Alice, to see the man who had run all the way to the hospital wearing green dinosaur-feet slippers and carrying a half-eaten sandwich.

'You great turnip,' said Alice's mum, smiling across the bed at her husband. 'You should have seen him, Alice. We were halfway through tea when the phone rang. He answered and next thing I knew, he'd dropped the phone and run out through the back door!'

The twins rolled together at the bottom of Alice's bed, shouting with laughter.

'Right through the town centre,' howled Kevin.

'Past all the market stalls,' hooted Gary.

'And the bus station!'

'And the—'

'All right, you two,' said Alice's dad. 'That's enough.'

'I had to pick the phone up off the floor to find out what was happening,' Alice's mum continued. 'If he'd only waited a few minutes, he could have come in the car with us.'

'I get a call saying my daughter has been taken to hospital in an ambulance and you expect me to wait a few minutes? Anyway,' he winked at Alice. 'I beat the car.'

'OK,' said the doctor, striding into the room. 'Less of the happy stuff, please. This is supposed to be a hospital.' She shone a pencil torch into Alice's eyes. 'Any headache?'

'No.'

'How many fingers?'

145

'Two.'

'What's your name?'

'Alice Mitchell.'

'What day is it?'

'Sunday.'

'What was your dad wearing on his feet yesterday?'

Alice giggled. 'Dinosaur-feet slippers. He still is. He hasn't been home all night.'

Solemnly Alice's dad raised his foot above the bed.

'Mmmm,' said the doctor. 'Claws too, I see.'

'Ah, but I did eat the sandwich.'

'All right, I think we've finished with you, Alice. As I told your mum and dad yesterday, you were out cold for quite a long time, but we can find absolutely nothing wrong with you. So we'll put it down to your fear of heights, shall we? Just don't climb any more ruined castles and we'll probably never see you, or your dad, again. Mr and Mrs Mitchell, do you want to come with me to the nurses' station to sign the discharge papers and collect her valuables?'

The twins went, too, and Alice, left

alone, lay back on the hard hospital bed and closed her eyes. She had not slept properly all night. The ward was too hot and the rubber undersheet had made her sweat and, whenever she did sleep, they kept waking her up to do their hourly observations. Alice could not wait to get home.

'Pssst!'

Alice jumped and opened her eyes. David, Frankie and Michael were hovering at the door. She took one look at them and burst into tears.

'Quick, Davey. Do your handkerchief bit,' said Frankie, hurrying to the side of the bed.

Alice giggled through her tears. 'Sorry. I keep doing this. I can't seem to stop.'

'Are your mom and dad mad at us?' asked Frankie.

'No.'

'OK. We'll stay then.' Frankie signalled to the boys to come in.

'Alice,' said Michael walking up to the bed and staring into her face. 'Don't ever do that to me again. I have never been as scared as I was at the top of those steps.'

'Why? What did I do?'

'What did you do? You nearly walked right over the edge of break-neck stairs with your eyes closed, that's all.' Michael shuddered. 'You actually had one foot stuck out over the drop when you fainted. Luckily you fell backwards, not forwards—'

'—And Michael acted as a human shied to stop you falling!' Frankie cut in.

'No, I did not. I just sat on the steps between you and the drop.'

'And Davey here made a cushion of his jacket for your head. Alice, I'm telling you, you had these guys at your command! Pity you were out cold.'

'Shut up, Frankie,' said David automatically, ducking his head and reaching over to straighten the corner of Alice's bed sheet. 'It's a good job you came round. It would've been my fault if you hadn't.'

'Why?' asked Alice.

'It was me who got the ambulance. See, we didn't know whether we should leave you on the stairs. We didn't know whether you'd be able to—you know— get back if someone moved you. But you

148

were out for so long, much longer than the other times, and then you started screaming about the worm.'

'Yeah, you were making the weirdest noises. Talk about scary!' Frankie gave a delighted shudder.

Alice remembered the blue flashing light she had seen at the top of the hill. 'I'm not sure, but I think I came back just as the ambulance arrived.'

'You should have seen those guys trying to get you down off the steps, then up the hill on a stretcher,' giggled Frankie.

'So, now it's your turn. What happened? Did you find Martha?' asked David.

'Yes,' said Alice. 'I did.' And she told them the whole story. When she had finished, there was a silence. Alice knew they were all still caught up in her description of Martha's death and the worm-train roaring through the castle wall. She sat quietly and waited.

At first she was puzzled by the strange little snuffling noise which finally broke the silence. She turned in the direction of the noise and her eyes grew wide with surprise. Tough, loud Frankie was crying. Wordlessly, Alice handed over David's handkerchief.

'I can't believe it,' snuffled Frankie. 'I can't believe she died. I thought she'd get away somehow. They always do, in the movies.'

'You can't edit the ending when it's real,' sighed David.

Frankie let out a wail and buried her face in the handkerchief. Awkwardly, David reached out and patted her on the shoulder.

'I'm so pleased she saw Tansy' said Michael, when Frankie had calmed down again.

'And I'm so pleased you were there yesterday to help me up those stairs,' said Alice. 'What was your dad like, when you got home?'

An expression of pain flickered across Michael's face. 'Oh well, the chess board was still set out, my lunch was still on the table and he wouldn't talk to me.' Michael shrugged and twisted his buttons. 'He still won't talk to me. It's not very nice. But, you know, even if I had stayed at home with him, I wouldn't

150

have made him happy. He hates the way I play chess. All these years I've kept trying to please him, I've never managed it. So, I'm glad I sneaked out on him. I'm glad I did it.'

'I couldn't have managed without you,' said Alice. 'Any of you.' She gave them all a wobbly smile.

'Time for a photograph,' said David, producing his polaroid camera.

'Hey! Great camera!' said Frankie, holding out her hand. 'Lemme see that.'

David sighed, looked down at his camera, then handed it over. Frankie stared at him, astonished.

'What? No instructions? No conditions?'

David shook his head.

'Hey, Davey. I think you're learning to live with me. Which is just as well. I've told my dad which school I want to go to. I start at your place tomorrow.' Frankie took her first shot, capturing David's expression of horror.

'That's great, Frankie!' said Alice.

Michael looked at David to see what he would say.

David grabbed back his camera and

151

jerked his head at Frankie's top, which was printed front and back with a coloured diagram showing the insides of a human body. 'At least you'll have to wear a uniform when you're at school,' he said.

'What, don't you like my hospital visiting t-shirt?' asked Frankie, pretending to be hurt.

David snorted and took a shot of Alice and Michael laughing together.

'Never mind,' said Frankie, brightening. 'Wait till you see what I can do with a school uniform. Hey, what's this for?' Frankie tugged on the flex that disappeared under Alice's pillow and pulled out a little box with a button in the middle of it.

'Don't press that!' shouted Alice, but she was too late.

'Hey, how was I to know it was a panic button?' grumbled Frankie, a few minutes later. She grinned at the doctor and Alice's family. 'It sure brought you running, though, didn't it?'

'Don't you know better than to push a button before you know what it's for? I'd throw you out if she wasn't going

152

anyway.' The doctor winked at Alice and stalked out of the room.

'They're letting you out?' asked David.

Alice nodded. 'I'm going home for a rest. I don't know how anybody ever gets any sleep in hospital.'

'Hey, how does this work?' Asked Frankie, sticking an oxygen mask over her face and fiddling with the cylinder.

'Out! Now!' yelled the doctor from the corridor. 'Anyone who isn't family, out!'

'Smile!' called David, taking one last polaroid shot of Alice and her family. 'Don't forget to time it,' he said, dropping the print on the bed and hurrying after Frankie and Michael.

Alice counted out the seconds, then peeled the cover from the photograph. The she was, sitting up in bed, with her mum on one side and her dad on the other. The twins were leaning over the bed in front of her, each waving one dinosaur-foot slipper in the air. They were all laughing.

'What a team!' said her dad, peering over her shoulder.

'What a family,' said Alice.